TONGUE TIED

The Donald Strachey Mysteries
by Richard Stevenson

Richard
Stevenson

TONGUE TIED

St. Martin's Minotaur
New York

www.minotaurbooks.com

Design by Nick Wunder

Library of Congress Cataloging-in-Publication Data

Stevenson, Richard, 1938–
    Tongue tied : a Donald Strachey mystery / Richard Stevenson.
        p. cm.
    ISBN 0-312-30974-0
    1. Strachey, Donald (Fictitious character)—Fiction. 2. Private
investigators—New York (State)—Albany—Fiction. 3. Radio
broadcasters—Fiction. 4. Albany (N.Y.)—Fiction. 5. Gay men—
Fiction. I. Title.

PS3569.T4567 T66 2003
813'.54—dc21

                                                           2002032999

First Edition: March 2003

10 9 8 7 6 5 4 3 2 1

This book is dedicated, with love and gratitude, to the Wheaton and Wheaton-Saines clan: Barbara, Bob, Henry, Melissa, Catherine, Phil, Brad, and Joe.

ACKNOWLEDGMENTS

Thanks to Zachary Lipez for Brooklyn, L-train party-car, and much other useful Fourteenth–to–Canal Street lore; to Frank Kelly for dope on Long Island locales; to Don Kilhefner for amazing stories on gay life among the Amish; and to the antic imagination of Joe Wheaton—he should win a prize—who invented Berkshire Woolly Llama Cheese.

TONGUE TIED

CHAPTER 1

The 24-across clue was " 'The Oblong Box' writer," and the answer was looming just over the hazy horizon of my Friday-morning mind when the man in the Amtrak seat next to me whipped out his cellphone, punched in some numbers, and announced, "Ed, it's Al."

I looked up from the folded-in-quarters arts section of the *Times* and said to the back of the seat ahead of me, "Ed, it's Al."

Missing just a fraction of a beat, Al said, "I'm on the train. I'll see Quinn when I get there, and I'm having lunch with Margaret Wills."

While Al listened to Ed's reply, I said, "I'm on the train. I'll see Quinn when I get there, and I'm having lunch with Margaret Wills."

Al peered over at me, and I peered back. Then he told Ed, "Listen, there's a guy in the seat next to me who . . ."

Like a simultaneous-translation whiz at the UN, I was right behind him. "Listen, there's a guy in the seat next to me who . . ."

I grinned as I said it, and Al's look of annoyance was turning to apprehension. This would make a good story when he met Quinn and then when he dined with Margaret Wills—"Would you believe, I was sitting next to this prick on the train who . . ."—but for now it must have been starting to seem to Al that I could be dangerous.

"Hang on a second," Al told Ed. He gathered up his laptop, flipped up and secured his tray table, stood, retrieved his nicely folded suit jacket from the overhead rack, and looked my way but avoided eye contact. He muttered, "Asshole," and strode up the aisle with his belongings.

Al found an aisle seat near the front of the car, where he disappeared from view if not entirely from earshot. Over the next few minutes, I still caught a word from time to time over the train's low whoosh and steady clickety-clack, although now Al was another unlucky passenger's voluble neighbor.

I went back to the crossword puzzle, but the "Oblong Box" writer's name was still beyond my reach. It was just three letters and should have been obvious. Amy Tan? Carolyn See? It didn't sound like either one. Myrna Loy? Eddie Foy? Not writers. I jumped down to 26-across: "spawn." Again, three letters. Kid? Doubtful. The *Times* puzzle makers could be slangy, but never imprecise.

I gazed out the window at the broad Hudson flying by, the blue Catskills hazy beyond the far shore. We sped south past a tanker pushing upstream to Albany, fuel for the state office workers' Subarus and minivans and the Pataki administration limos. A shirtless man and a woman wearing a green halter and red headband paddled downriver in a yellow canoe closer in to the near shore. The mountains across the water lolled like hippos in the July sun.

Another couple of words flew back from noisy Al, and I wondered how long it would take before Amtrak felt enough customer pressure and segregated cellphone yakkers the way it once had smokers. Would mounting numbers of letters and phone calls do it, or would a media-worthy "incident" trigger the regulations? *Poughkeepsie—A Schenectady man was roughed up by three Amtrak passengers, and his cellular telephone flushed down the lavatory toilet by a fourth.* . . .

Or would public cellphone high-decibel palaver come to be seen as a First Amendment issue, with the Supreme Court forced eventually to rule on what ought to be a question not of constitutional law but of manners, and with the ACLU left in the awkward position of defending not endangered free speech but mere pains in the ass?

The question of genuine social harm versus simple obnoxiousness was of more than passing interest to me, for I was about to—maybe—take on as a client a man six or eight million Americans considered an exhilarating breath of fresh air, while others—I was one—thought of him as, if not a social menace, then certainly a tiresome gasbag.

Like cellphone boorishness, the caustic iconoclasm of Jay Plankton—"the J-Bird" to his radio fans—seemed to me a social phenomenon to be avoided but no threat to the republic. I even knew intelligent and perfectly sane people who found Plankton delightful—none of them black or gay, although more of them women than I could readily comprehend.

And unlike Howard Stern and Rush Limbaugh, both basically entertainers with a crude gimmick—bathroom and sex jokes in the one case, inflaming hinterland right-wingers in the other—the J-Bird actually seemed to hold convictions, however confused and ill-informed. He regularly lured public figures, sometimes elected officials, onto his 7-to-10-A.M. show, where they spoke more candidly—or at least with a more shrewd approximation of candor—than they did in other public venues. And they engaged in the uniquely American form of humor that's the democratic alternative to Shavian wit, guys joshing one another.

Plankton did, however, maintain such a gift for sour invective—people he didn't like were "diseased toads" and "maggot mouths" and "lying sacks of bull puke"—that some of his targets or their admirers occasionally became furious. And his rants, egged on by an on-air claque of like-minded but less talented men whose job opportunities else-where might have been limited, sometimes even triggered physical threats against the J-Bird.

That's where I came in. Plankton's producer had learned of a minor encounter I'd once had with a radical group, the Forces of Free Faggotry, that had been making the J-Bird's life miserable for several months and now threatened to make it even worse. Would I, could I, go to work for this man? Maybe not, although I was curious to learn what the FFF was up to, and of course to get a firsthand look at a widely popular man I couldn't stand. So here I was, headed south at seventy-eight miles an hour, eight seats back from Al, and flummoxed by 24-across.

The FFF, I thought, had fallen apart sometime in the seventies. And yet apparently it was back, a band of self-described queer revolutionaries in the era of *Will & Grace*. The cognitive dissonance was considerable—or would have been if I hadn't listened to the J-Bird's show the day before and renewed my appreciation of how this guy might inspire violent rage in some people.

The FFF had not been violent in its earlier incarnation; in the late sixties and early seventies the group specialized in rescuing young gays and lesbians from mental institu-tions their parents had put them in to have them "cured" of their homosexuality. The FFF had employed brash and sometimes illegal methods, but all the viciousness had been on the other side. It seemed unlikely that the old FFFers had at this late date turned into cryptoterrorists—most revolutionaries mellow in middle age—but the J-Bird seemed to think they had.

I gave the crossword puzzle a rest from its exertions, and by the time I made my way back to my seat with a foam cup of Amtrak's extraordinarily rich and flavorful coffee, the train, due in at Penn Station in forty minutes, was close enough to the city for me to pick up the J-Bird's show on Timothy Callahan's radio.

This was the radio with earphones that Timmy used when he lounged on the deck behind our Crow Street house in Albany on warm summer Friday evenings to listen to the concerts broadcast from Tanglewood. He used the earphones because, he said, the neighbors might not be as crazy about Schumann as he was. In his consideration for others, an admirable anachronism was Callahan. Of course, he also relied on the earphones to mask the sounds of neighbors with stereos who were more in tune with the times than he was, and of the carrying-on around our kitchen table whenever I could lure in the elderly lesbian couple who lived two doors down the street for a raucous game of hearts.

"Gore is ridiculous, just *ridiculous*, and that . . . that smirking, no-good weasel Bush is no better . . ." The J-Bird was in hyperrant, his famous barroom-loudmouth-at-2-A.M. slurred snarl at full throttle. "I might not vote *at all*. I might just . . . *leave the country* before I pull the switch for either one of those two . . . *sorry losers*."

To the approving chortles of his studio buddies—the newsreader, the sports reporter, and two other attendants whose roles were murkier—Plankton fumed on. He had supported John McCain and Bill Bradley in the spring primaries, and the J-Bird was beside himself with frustration over the electorate's having been left to choose between the two unworthies, George Bush and Al Gore. That the policy ideas of McCain, a conservative on every subject except campaign finance, and of Bradley, the largely unreconstructed liberal, were diametrically opposed was of no concern to Plankton, who seemed to judge people not by their ideas, or even their behavior necessarily, but by their degree of "guyness."

Guyness to the J-Bird mainly meant a style built around hurling insults, usually involving physical characteristics, at people who enjoyed the abuse—or at people who didn't like it at all and when they said so could be called "politically correct" whiners. People like Bradley, who didn't necessarily relish this form of discourse but good-naturedly went along with it, were okay guys too. It helped that Bradley was tall. Short was bad and fat even worse. Despite the antigay tone of the show—one of the hangers-on crooned and lisped whenever the subject came up—the weird obsession with weight and body shape on the J-Bird show was reminiscent of a bevy of West Hollywood gym queens. It was one of the show's odder inconsistencies.

On this Friday morning, the J-Bird blustered on about the deficiencies of George W. Bush—who affected guyness but who was such a privileged brat that his guyness was inauthentic and therefore beneath contempt—and of Al Gore, who was regarded as plastic and slippery and not nearly rough-hewn enough, despite his having been to war and back, an opportunity for guyness that the J-Bird had chosen to forgo.

"Having to pick between these two sniveling pipsqueaks sucks, it just sucks!" the J-Bird sputtered on. "And Nader—*he's* no better. That priss, that whiner. Although at least he's got some guts. He did take on . . . back in the sixties . . . who was it? Was it Chrysler?"

"It was General Motors," the newsreader put in.

"General Motors, then."

"Rear-end collisions on the . . . what was it? The Corvair? The Pinto?"

"A pinto's not a car; it's a bean," the J-Bird said.

"The musical fruit."

"Like Elton John," came another voice, one of the J-Bird's Greek chorus.

"What?" The J-Bird didn't get it at first.

"Elton John, the musical fruit." More chuckles all around.

"Is *he* running for president? He couldn't be any worse than the pathetic bozos we have to pick from now."

"I do tholemnly thwear, Mary, that I will uphold the Conthituthun . . ."

This brought cackles, and I had just about decided to skip the meeting with Plankton, have a pleasant lunch in the park, and board the next train back to Albany, when the laughter on the radio suddenly stopped.

"Hey, what the eff . . . !" It was Plankton's voice, but then it was gone too, and a commercial came on for a New Jersey Toyota dealer. This was followed by a short silence, then a second ad, and a third. Then the J-Bird returned briefly—from another studio, he said—to announce that the rest of the day's show would be a recording of an earlier show, and he would explain it all the following Monday. It was hard to understand all of the J-Bird's words, for he seemed to be choking.

CHAPTER 2

A big *FFF* had been spray-painted in red on the main doors of the Thirtieth Street office building that housed the radio station where the J-Bird's show originated. When I arrived, just after 10:30, two NYPD cruisers were double-parked out front, along with an ambulance, flashers flashing. The 10 A.M. news on the J-Bird station had reported that a tear-gas canister had been lobbed into the J-Bird's studio by a man disguised as a police officer, and in the confusion the man had escaped. Plankton and his on- and off-air staff had quickly fled the studio, been treated by paramedics who soon arrived on the scene, and avoided serious injury. Gas for the gaseous, I thought.

A security guard in the lobby stopped me and said no one was being allowed access to the sixth floor of the build-

ing. But my New York State private investigator's ID cou-
pled with a phone call to Plankton's office got me into the
elevator, which was operated by another armed security
officer. It smelled of tear gas, sharp and sour.

Two uniformed city cops stood in the small lobby of the
station. One of them consulted with the receptionist—her
name tag read "Flonderee"—who made a call into the inner
recesses. Soon a portly balding man of forty or so, not much
over five feet, wearing khakis, Top-Siders, and a navy blue
golf shirt emerged, and I said, "Hi, I'm Don Strachey. Are
you the J-Bird?"

No, he said, he was Jay Plankton's producer, Horace
"Call me Jerry" Jeris. He led me down a long corridor, away
from an open window where an industrial-size fan was ven-
tilating the place, which still reeked.

"Lemme bring you up to speed before Jay pops in,"
Jeris said, ushering me into an office modest in its size and
appointments for a man of Jeris's position in America's cultural life. "Jay'll be glad to see you after this latest fuck-all.
You heard what happened?"

"I was listening on the train. And I can smell it."

"I didn't take a direct hit myself, but the guys in the
studio did. You ever been teargassed, Don? It's a bitch."

"I was once. After I got back from the Johnson-Nixon-
Kissinger war, which I helped out with in a small way, I
joined other people with similar experiences in publicly
pointing out that we'd had a serious change of heart about
the whole thing. For our trouble, we were gassed."

"No shit?"

"Although the home-front war didn't compare with the
real thing. Don't get me wrong."

Jeris opened up a humidor on his desk and offered me a
cigar the size of a Yule log. I didn't stammer out, "I would
rather inhale the tear-gas fumes than the stench from that
grotesque stomach pump," but just said no thanks. Jeris
embarked upon the ritual of the cigar, and I seated myself

in a canvas director's chair with *The J-Bird* stitched across the back.

"Now you've got an idea what we're up against," Jeris said. "When these FFF jerk-offs started out, they were pains in the ass, but it wasn't like they were actually gonna hurt anybody. They mailed us turds and cow brains and crap, and Jay even thought some of it was funny. But now we're into this shit. Jay hates to do it, but it looks like he's gonna have to have a bodyguard to actually follow him around. He's got good security in his building, and we thought we were safe here at the station too, but today we really got fucked over by these crud."

I said, "That's not what you have in mind for me, I guess. My expertise is limited in security work, and I don't do it."

"Nah. It's your connections with these FFF guys we're interested in. It's this NYPD detective, Lyle Barner, who says he knew you when he was a cop in Albany. He says you tracked down a gay kid after his asshole parents put him in the bin, and it was the FFF that helped him escape."

"The chronology's a little off," I said. "But I did use the FFF to locate a young man named Billy Blount, who was wanted on a phony murder charge. This was twenty years ago, though, and I'd find it hard to believe that any of the FFF are still around. They broke up as a group even before I met one of them in Denver, around seventy-nine. My guess is, the Forces of Free Faggotry gang that's giving Plankton a hard time is another outfit entirely. They probably heard about the old FFF and picked up on the name. I doubt that an old radical group's name can be copyrighted."

Jeris examined the smoldering cigar thoughtfully. The stench from the thing was awful. Cigars had once held a romance for me; they evoked happy childhood memories of trips from central New Jersey to Phillies or Yankees games on a Pennsylvania Railroad smoker with my dad and his cronies. But that was long ago, and now it was all I could do to keep from saying, "Jerry, since you're smoking that cigar, do you mind if I drop my pants, bend over, and light farts while we're chatting?"

Instead, I said, "Doesn't the NYPD have any leads at all? If the harassment has been going on steadily for weeks, they must have more to go on than anything I'm likely to come up with from my brief, now-stale contact with the FFF."

"Yeah, you'd think they'd be on top of it by now," Jeris said. "And Jay has plenty of fans in the department, so it isn't like they're blowing us off. But until today the FFF pretty much mailed in all the shit—and I do mean shit—so there wasn't any physical evidence that was traceable. I'd show you some of the disgusting doo-doo they sent Jay, but the cops have it all. Call Lyle Barner, and he'll give you the tour."

"Well, I wouldn't mind catching up with Lyle."

"The thing is, Don, while Jay is concerned, naturally, he is far from being intimidated. Which I'm sure you can appreciate from listening to his show. Or," Jeris said with a derisive snort, "are you the NPR type? The travails of poets in Egypt and all that elitist crap?"

"I've heard Plankton's show," I said, and glanced at the digital clock above Jeris's computer terminal. When was the next train back to Albany? Was it noon or one o'clock? Noon would be cutting it close, one o'clock no problem. Just pick up a deli sandwich, go back to "The Oblong Box"—Karla Jay? Robb Forman Dew?—and be back in Albany by midafternoon, never again to lay eyes on these people.

"I know you're gay," Jeris said next. "And I just want you to know, that's no problem for us."

"Praise be."

"That on-air shit is just . . . Jay can't stand political correctness. You gotta admit, Don, that's fair enough."

I said, "What if I chased these new FFF guys down and then I decided to join them in making the J-Bird's life a living hell? Which, by the way, is how you described it on the phone yesterday."

"That's because of the threats, not the juvenile pranksterism. The note with the last mailing said things were gonna get worse. And today things did."

"But maybe these people—whoever they are—maybe they'll convince me that the J-Bird deserves all the grief he's getting from them. That he deserves that and worse. That all the adolescent fag-baiting on the show encourages bullies and bashers, and it's not only dumb and tedious, but dangerous too. Maybe I'll find the FFF, and they'll recruit me, and I'll come after the J-Bird, and you'll rue the day you ever brought me into this. Then what?"

"Then," Jeris said, blowing a smoke ring, "I'd have to ask for our money back. What is your fee scale, anyway? Can we afford you? This isn't Albany, with all that lobbyist funny money sloshing around."

I told him what my normal fee was, mentally calculating an extra twenty-five percent and adding it in.

"That's outside our budget," Jeris said, and he suggested a figure twenty-five percent lower than what I'd told him. I shrugged, and he said, "We'll work something out."

"Jerry, you said on the phone yesterday that if I could locate the FFF people, you wouldn't necessarily want to prosecute them; you'd just want to talk to them. This makes me wonder. It reminds me of the Blount case twenty years ago, when the parents of Billy Blount hired me to bring their wanted-for-murder son back to Albany and turn him over, not to the police, but to them. As it happened, these people were as duplicitous as anybody I've ever done business with. They were the abysmal dregs."

"Nah, we'll play it straight with you," Jeris said, waving away doubt with his cigar. "We don't want to chop these guys' balls off, we just want to work something out with them so they'll get off Jay's case. They want us to can Leo Moyle, and we're not gonna do that. But we can talk to them, I'm sure of it. Jay thinks it would be fun to put them on the air."

"Moyle is the resident gay-baiter?"

"Leo is kind of a loose cannon, yeah. But that's what's so great about him. He lends the show an element of danger. I don't go along with half of what he comes out with, and speaking candidly, neither does Jay. But you gotta have an un-PC presence on any show today, or your show is gonna be shit-canned faster than you can say Phil Donahue. Leo stays; that's a given. But can we talk to these FFFers, maybe give them their fifteen minutes, let them promote the glories of cocksucking or whatever? I think we can work it out. Anyway, let's track them down and see exactly what it is that we've got to work with here."

It all sounded unlikely to me—as unlikely as LBJ inviting the Chicago Seven in for bourbon and branch water and a tête-à-tête with Bob McNamara and the Joint Chiefs of Staff. I said, "Doesn't Plankton put only people he likes on the show? People he basically agrees with, or at least gets along with? The show's not *Crossfire* or *The McLaughlin Group*. He's never been interested in a cross section of viewpoints before, as far as I'm aware."

"Not true," Jeris said, through an expanding toxic cloud. "Jay likes badass people if they're real, no matter where they're coming from politically or whatever. Especially if they're funny badass real. Funny and not phony are what Jay looks for and what our listeners tune in for. These FFFers are deeply sincere, apparently, and they're crude as shit, for chrissakes, so . . . no, there's no problem with them getting on the air. We'd do a pre-interview, naturally, to make sure they can express themselves verbally as effectively as they send fecal matter through the US Postal Service."

"They sent actual shit? Not a joke-shop rendition?"

"Some kind of animal turds," Jeris said, opening a folder next to his computer and handing me several sheets of paper. "NYPD has the stuff at a lab for analysis. Here's a list of what's come in to us so far, and photocopies of the notes that came with it."

The first page, a word-processor printout, contained a list of dates and notations for each date. For June 2, the notation was *Asswipe for the homophobic asshole* and, in parentheses, *Rover break-in*. The other dates, beginning with June 9 and ending on July 7, were followed by these notations: *brains for the brainless; charms for the charmless; douche for the douche bag; excrement for the execrable; fat for the fathead*.

I said, "What does 'Rover break-in' mean?"

"They hit Jay's Range Rover," Jeris said. "This was the first incident. They broke into the Rover while it was parked outside Jay's agent's house in Westchester and filled it with unrolled toilet paper."

"Clean toilet paper?"

"Mercifully. They left a note that said, 'Asswipe for the homophobic asshole, from the Forces of Free Faggotry.' "

"Did the local cops investigate?"

"This was in Mamaroneck, and the local constables did what they could, apparently, but they came up empty. A major party was on in the house, and it might have been a little noisy in the neighborhood. So nobody saw or heard anything. We can't figure how they could have known Jay was going to be at a party that night at Mark Krentzman's house, so we think the FFFers must have followed Jay up from the city."

"I suppose," I said, "that as soon as Plankton saw the intended victim of the prank was designated an 'asshole,' he understood right away that his being the target was no case of mistaken identity."

Showing no indication of being either insulted or amused, Jeris said, "A lot of people can't stand Jay. We all know that. You take on the PC crowd, trouble's gonna come boogalooing your way. It's a given. These are the most humorless people on earth."

"Except for the hilarious FFF, of course. You said Plankton thinks they're funny. But this stuff isn't funny. It's just dopey and crude."

Jeris blew smoke and shrugged.

What were Jeris and the J-Bird up to? None of this added up. Unless, of course, Plankton, Jeris, and their gang truly saw the adolescent-boy antics of the neo-FFF as representing their own level of thinking and style of expression—spreading noxious materials through the mails or over the airwaves, literally or metaphorically—and considered their harassers as a special variety of brothers under the skin. "Guys," of a sort, that they could talk to, do business with, lob crass, jolly insults back and forth with. But that sounded either too naive for the J-Bird's crew or maybe not naive enough. Jeris seemed less spontaneous than calculating on other matters, so why not on this one too?

I said, "Then after the toilet-paper episode, foul substances began showing up in the mail?"

"Cow brains, animal turds, a pound of rancid lard stuffed in a freezer bag. Also some unknown fluid in a jar that we didn't really want to find out what it was. In the middle of all this, on June sixteenth, we received the first real communication we'd had from these people besides the descriptive labels. And that's the letter telling us what the FFF is, and how they're gonna wipe out homophobia, et cetera, et cetera, and they'll leave us alone if we dump Leo. The letter was hard to decipher because it had some kind of gummy orange candy smeared all over it."

"Lucky Charms for the unlucky charmless?"

"That was it. You've got a copy of the note right there, minus the gumdrops."

The letter, also typed on a word processor and dated June 16, had no signature. It read:

J-Bird—
You are now operating under the watchful eye of the Forces of Free Faggotry. We intend to rid the US air-

*waves of homophobia. Your show is first. If you want us
to leave you alone, eliminate Leo and all other traces of
homophobia from your show. Reason has no effect on
people like you. But other means will. We have only gotten
started. It's a long alphabet. If you make it to Z and
think you are home free, think again. We'll just start over.
So act now.*

I flipped to the final page, a copy of a note that arrived
the day before, July 13. It said only:

*For your own good, wait no longer. Meet our demands or
someone will be hurt.*

Your regular listeners—
The FFF

I said, "You're really going to put these people on the
air? They sound demented. However worthy the FFF's
aims, they sound a little . . . way out there."

"S'okay by us," Jeris said mildly. "We're not Jerry
Springer, but we're not Oprah either. Edge is a big part of
what Jay is about. We'll do it by phone so we don't have to
nail the chairs to the floor. It won't feed the starving in
Africa, but it'll be great radio. It'll be real."

"What if these FFF guys won't cooperate?" I asked.
"They sound to me like true believers who are fixated on one
thing, which is purging J-Bird's show of juvenile fag-baiting,
and that's the one thing that's least likely to happen."

"Hey, who knows?" Jeris said brightly. "Maybe the J-
Bird is a closeted gay, and he'll take this opportunity to
come out of the closet and shit-can Leo on the air. I told you
Jay likes to push the envelope."

As Jeris said this, the door to the corridor opened, and a
big, potbellied man in shades and with a head of Brillo-pad
hair stood there. In unmistakable tones, he said, "Are you

the gay gumshoe from Albany? Christ, you're not even wearing a dress."

I got up, walked over to the J-Bird, lifted his shades off his ample red nose, and said, "Isn't there something you'd like to talk to me about, Jay? You look as though you've been weeping."

CHAPTER 3

Soon Jeris and the J-Bird were both going at it, and I was obliged to get up and open a window. Jeris had no objection, but Plankton called me a wuss. I'd have mewed out something about the high risks among cigar smokers of mouth, throat, and larynx cancer, but these guys weren't about health, or even survival; they were about "edge."

This was an impulse I understood. In the seventies and early eighties I had escaped HIV only through the dumbest luck, although gleeful coupling with another human being still seemed a far worthier way to risk one's life than voluntarily inhaling a substance that would lead the average well-trained firefighter to reach for oxygen. Comparing notes in these areas with Jeris and the J-Bird, however, felt as though it might not be productive, so I stuck to the topic of my possible employment.

"Jerry tells me you'd like to put the FFF on the air," I told Plankton, who was lounging on the office couch, his cowboy-booted feet on the coffee table. He had the cigar in one beefy hand, a can of Sprite in the other, and he still had the shades on. He wore baggy khakis and a beige sports shirt, garb Al Gore's most recent wardrobe adviser might have selected, generating catcalls among the J-Bird set.

"It remains to be seen," Plankton snarled, "whether they'll go on the show or whether I'll have them put away in effing Leavenworth. After today, they probably ought to have their sorry butts kicked from here to Bridgeport. Just put us in touch with them, and then we'll see what happens next. We don't have to look at their ugly faces. Christ, just the idea of sitting down across from these perverts makes me want to lose my breakfast."

"If you want me to work for you," I said, "don't call gay people perverts in my presence. Don't say it on the air either when I'm listening to the show. And since you won't know when I'm listening and when I'm not, you might want to err on the side of caution."

"Jesus!" Plankton spat out, shaking his head. "Is dealing with you and your oh-I'm-so-sensitive, limp-wristed, politically correct horseshit what I'm going to have to put up with in order to get these sickos off my back? They threatened me, you know. They physically threatened me. I'm doing them an effing favor bringing you into it instead of the goddamn FBI."

Jeris said, "How would you like us to refer to the FFF people, Don? Do you want us to call them 'homosexual gentlemen'?"

Plankton said, "Or how about 'Froot Loops'?"

Were they testing me, or provoking me, or what? I supposed there was nothing calculated, or even rational, about this routine at all. It was just the way they talked to other men. They didn't know any other way. Or, they were capable of nonhostile, noninflammatory, straightforward conversation, but—with me—only one-on-one. When they were together, they had to lay on a barrage of "guy" talk in order to keep their heterosexual credentials from being questioned, however subtly or obliquely, and this seemed to mean nearly as much to them as life itself.

I said, "If I take you on as a client, every time you say something that irritates me, there's going to be a surcharge on my normal fee of two percent. You work it out. Or, I can walk out the door now and you can take your chances that the New York cops will collar the FFF people before they send you another load of dogshit, or worse."

"Llama," Plankton interrupted.

"Llama?"

"I was just on the phone with that police dick, Lyle Barner. He said the turds they sent us—'excrement for the execrable'—were tested somewhere, and they're llama crap."

"These guys must be Aztecs," Jeris said, his geography off by several thousand miles.

"I loved 'excrement for the execrable,' " Plankton said, and laughed. "I wish I'd thought of that one myself."

"You will," Jeris said, and they both chuckled.

"You should be on the radio too," I told Jeris. "You're almost as funny as Jay is." They both haw-hawed at this; now I was getting into the J-Bird spirit. I asked Plankton, "What else did you learn from Lyle Barner that's new?"

Plankton drew on his cigar and blew smoke, and I wondered if I was going to be able to keep my Amtrak cherry Danish down. "Nada," he said. "Barner's on his way over here to talk to us about the tear-gas attack, and he says he wants you to stick around so he can talk to you."

"Did the fake cop who lobbed the canister leave a note?" I asked.

"Just the usual wiseass label, in an envelope he dropped on Flonderee's desk. This one said, 'Gas for the gaseous.'"

"I could have written it myself. It's the phrase I thought of when I heard about the tear-gas incident. I'd just been listening to your show, and it was the first thought that came into my head."

"You're an effing genius," Plankton said. I couldn't see his bloodshot eyes through the shades, but a couple of gray-black brushpiles of eyebrow shot up. "Since you're so smart, why don't you tell us what the *H* incident is going to be? What do you think, Don? Will it be . . . what? Hay for the heinous?"

"How about 'Hogs for the hogs-breathed'?" Jeris said. "Or 'Hemorrhoids for the hemorrhoidal'?"

Laughing and coughing up a merry storm, Plankton sputtered out, "What about 'hoors for the hoor-ible'? That wouldn't be too hard to take," he said, and Jeris coughed and cackled too.

They quickly collected themselves when I said, "Maybe it'll be 'homicide for the homophobic.'"

Plankton set down his soft drink, removed his shades, and gazed at me through the air pollution with deep-set red eyes that once must have been blue. "You don't think they're really that dangerous, do you? They're out of control, sure. That's why we brought the cops into it, and that's why we called you. But now you're starting to scare the bejesus out of me."

I shrugged. "These people are not without humor, but they're also a bit nuts. How nuts, we don't know. You and the people on your show are out of control too," I said to Plankton, "but you're not homicidal that anybody knows of. So, surly and obnoxious and frightening to some people is sometimes just that and nothing worse."

Jeris said to Plankton, "That's a compliment, J-Bird."

"Oh? I'm not so sure it is," Plankton said, and slid his shades back on.

I said, "So you're bringing on personal security for yourself? That's a useful precaution at this point."

"Two of them are in my office now. It's a service Lyle Barner knew about—ex-cops—and, Christ, they look like a couple of World Wrestling Federation bone-crunchers. What a pain in the effing butt this is," Plankton said, and flicked a cigar ash in his soda can.

"You afraid the Secret Service might crimp your style, J-Bird?" Jeris asked. "Hey, it didn't slow Bubba down."

"Are you single?" I asked Plankton.

"Divorced. Twice. Three kids, all adults—or about as adult as any kids are these days."

I only thought it, but Jeris said it out loud. "That's hard to believe, with a role model like you, Jay." They snickered together companionably.

I asked, "Is there anybody you live with or are close to that the FFF might go after?"

"I live by myself. I have an apartment on Sixty-fourth, off Lex." Plankton said to Jeris, "Jesus, I hope they don't try to do anything to Babette. Cripes."

I was ashamed of myself as soon as it came out. "Who's Babette, J-Bird? Your poodle?"

This was their style of wit, and they both heh-hehed.

"Babette's a bitch," Plankton said, "but . . ."

Jeris finished his sentence. ". . . but not nearly the bitches that Gail and Theresa were!"

More happy chortles, more fumes. As my gorge was rising, my heart was sinking. The gay-baiting was bad enough, but this casual misogyny was even worse. They sneered at gay people to their faces, but my guess was that they put their girlfriends down in this contemptible way only behind their backs. Or, worse, they carried on like this in front of their girlfriends, who suffered through it all as part of some awful bargain they believed they had had to make, and maybe they were right. I needed the work at the time—Albany in the past month had apparently experienced an uncharacteristic outbreak of decorum, so my services had been in limited demand. But it seemed likelier by the second that I would not be able to abide any association whatsoever, even for an inflated fee, with the J-Bird and company. I knew I would be seeing Lyle Barner within minutes, and I decided I would break the news first to him that I was soon to be gone.

CHAPTER 4

"Long time, no see," Barner said. "Looks like you're not twenty-six anymore, Strachey."

"Thank you."

"But you're as sexy as ever. How do you do it?"

"Ingest lots of grease, put off going to the gym, not too much bed rest."

"Funny, I try some of that. But for me it doesn't work so well."

"You can't do slovenliness halfheartedly, Lyle. You've got to give it your all."

He laughed, a little nervously, and glanced at the door to make sure, I guessed, that it was shut tight and no one had overheard this exchange. Jeris had let us use his office for a private confab following Detective Barner's official tour of the tear gas–attack area.

It had been nearly sixteen years since I'd last laid eyes on Barner, and he hadn't aged as badly as apparently he thought he had. Beefy, with powerful shoulders and arms, a broad mug, and big sad brown eyes, Barner had what was once called a "man's man" way about him that still had its potent appeal. I'd had a couple of sexual encounters with Barner in the early eighties, back when Timothy Callahan and I had already gotten serious with each other but the angel of monogamy had not yet appeared before us, at least not to me.

Barner had been interested in me at the time, and for me there was the sinful thrill that came with Barner's vague resemblance to my high-school football coach. But his essentially morose nature, as well as his terror of being outed as an Albany gay cop, was a source of tension between us. And anyway Timmy was arguing for a more conventional straight-and-narrow relationship between us, both out of a well-founded fear of AIDS and because it was his moral ideal; he had always been both selective and definite in what he retained during his early years with the nuns of Poughkeepsie, as well as in his later years at Georgetown, where the free flow of ideas was revered by the Jesuits there and where on every classroom wall hung a crucifix.

In an attempt to integrate his divided selves, and partly at my urging, Barner had headed for San Francisco in the mid-eighties; it was easier out there for cops to be uncloseted. But instead I'd heard he'd married a divorcée with six kids. That hadn't worked either, I was not bowled over to learn later. And the rumor I'd picked up in the mid-nineties, that Barner was back east with the NYPD, was now confirmed.

I said, "I thought once you'd cut the cord with Mother Albany and discovered the moist charms of life in the Bay area, I'd never see you again. Or that if I did, you'd have flowers in your hair."

"I had to come back east because my ma's not well," Barner said simply.

"Sorry to hear it. Your mother's here in the city?"

"No, Albany."

"But no back-to-your-roots for you?"

"It wouldn't work."

"I guess not. Albany city government is no longer stuck in the nineteen-thirties. It hasn't been since the eighties. But the Neanderthals have managed to retain the law-enforcement and criminal-justice portfolios. I can't see an out gay cop fitting in comfortably. Although I'd love to see some ballsy young gay guy break the mold."

Barner said coldly, "That's right, Strachey. You'd like to see somebody else stand up and take a pounding. But you never stood up yourself, did you?"

"Become a cop, you mean?"

"It's a hell of a lot harder than what you do, and it's more important."

"When it's done right, which it rarely is, that's true. But I don't fit into institutions very well, as is documented in the archives of the Pentagon."

"Then maybe you should keep your fucking mouth shut about cops being out."

I said, "I take it you're not."

He shook his head.

"And it's gnawing at you?"

"No, *you're* gnawing at me, that's all."

"Lyle, I haven't knowingly been within a couple of thousand miles of you for over fifteen years, for chrissakes." Déjà vu was setting in. This sounded like a repeat of half the conversations I'd ever had with Barner.

"That's right, Strachey. You haven't spoken to me for sixteen years. And as soon as you do, you start right in again."

"Are you in a relationship?" I asked.

He hesitated. "Yes. Kind of one."

"A cop?"

"Yeah."

"Ah-ha."

"He's out."

"Oh-ho."

Barner's look softened, and he said, "I'm totally wacko nuts about Dave, and I'm afraid I'm going to lose him. He's in the Gay Officers Action League. He wants me out too, so we can do that political stuff together. But he's treated like crap by three-quarters of the officers in the precinct, and he can hardly do his job. I love my job, I'm good at it, and I don't want to get up every day and have to wade through that shit while I'm just trying to go out and be an effective police officer."

I said, "Dave is a hero. The only people marching in gay-pride parades who get as many cheers from the crowd as P-FLAG does are the out gay cops."

Barner flushed and looked at me hard. "There are *other* ways of being a hero. Some people might say trying your damnedest twelve hours a day to protect the public from the half a million or so sociopaths and violent nutcases loose on the streets of this city—and instead of being thanked for it getting called racists and out-of-control assholes—is being a hero too. That's how *I'm* a hero, when I feel like one, and a hell of a lot of other good cops are heroes like that too. So you tell me, Strachey. What's wrong with *that* kind of being a hero?"

This was an argument that I knew tripped off the tongues of racist, corrupt and sadistically depraved cops as casually as it did among cops for whom it was essentially true. I was reasonably certain that Barner was one of the latter, and I said, "I respect you and what you do, Lyle. I remember what a fine cop you were in Albany—you bailed my ass out with that maniac who chewed my ear off in the

Millpond case—and I'll bet you're an even better cop now. I wasn't putting you down. I was only suggesting that you've got a real prize of a boyfriend."

Now Barner looked thoughtful, and said, "Are you still with that Irish kid?"

Timmy would love this. "Timothy Callahan, yes. But if that's who you're thinking of, he was an adult sixteen years ago, and he's even more of one now."

"I figured it would last."

"We've had our ups and downs. But we're in it for the long haul. Our differences drive us both nuts sometimes, but we complete each other in an interestingly asymmetrical way. Plus, we still get each other's pulses racing somewhat more often than you might think. It's definitely a marriage made in purgatory, as all the best ones are. Somebody once accused us of being the Ozzie and Harriet of gay Albany, and Timmy took it as a compliment."

Barner seemed to mull this over; then he said, "I'd like you to meet Dave."

"I'd like to. Is he a detective too?"

"Patrolman."

"I see. How old?"

"Twenty-six. He's mature."

"And has mature tastes, which is even better."

"He's a hunk, Strachey."

"That's no handicap either."

"In some ways I wish I could be more like him. But I can't."

"Does he expect you to become more like him?"

Barner thought this over. "He'd definitely prefer it," he said after a moment. "But he knows I'm set in my ways. He knows it, but he doesn't accept it. That's the problem, if you see what I mean. I don't know how long he's gonna stick around."

"It's as tricky as anything," I said. "A couple can be out, or a couple can be in. But when one person's in and the other person's out, the picture can get a little too abstract-expressionistic for most people to handle. I hope you can figure out a way to make it work, if you both want to."

"It might. Dave likes me. He thinks I'm a good cop, and smart—and hot."

"That was my impression."

Barner said, "The thing that gets to me is, he sees other guys sometimes."

"Oh. And you don't?"

"Nah."

"That is definitely another complication."

"Yeah."

"Hmm."

"We spend most of our time together when we're off duty. So these other guys—mostly they're not an issue."

"What do you like to do together, you and Dave? I mean generally speaking."

"Watch Yankee games, have a beer, go out for a nice meal, get it on. You know."

I said, "I take it you're not out with anybody except your close friends?"

"Correct."

"And not these bozos here at the radio station? I shouldn't address you as 'Detective Mary Mary Quite Contrary' in the presence of the J-Bird?"

"Jesus!"

"How did you end up detective in charge of the FFF case? Luck of the draw?"

Barner allowed himself a sly little grin. "I requested it. I remembered the Blount case in seventy-nine, and that you had FFF connections. I thought I might be able to bring you into it."

"And here I am, although not for long, I think. The J-Bird and his gang of boneheads are not people I want to work for. If this were North Korea and my family were starving, I'd have to think it over. Thankfully, that's not the case. Sorry to crap out on you, but I think I'm about to head back north."

Barner looked puzzled. "You don't want to take money from these people? You think these people's money is dirtier than anybody else's? You're pretty fucking idealistic for somebody your age, Strachey. You need to get out in the big bad world more often. You must have been stuck up in Albany a little too long."

"Lyle, it's not my ideals I'm afraid of losing, it's my breakfast. And my temper."

"Uh-huh."

"It's been awhile since I've had to restrain myself from decking a client."

Barner laughed. "Jesus, Strachey, I know caterers who put up with more obnoxious clients than Plankton and Jerry Jeris. Why don't you hang in for a few days anyway? Take the J-Bird's money, and find out what you can about the old FFF. It'll be interesting, and it'll make my life easier. Do it as a favor to me. I don't want to come right out and say that you owe me one. But if you keep this up, I might have to." He looked at me and waited.

I felt my pleasant postlunch train ride back to Albany begin to slip away. Barner had once saved my neck, if not my ear, in a case involving the two elderly lesbians who were now Timmy's and my neighbors on Crow Street. A developer trying to drive them out of their semirural home near Albany had set in motion a plot that led to a violent confrontation with two murderous goons and a vicious dog, and it was Barner who had arrived on the scene accompanied by Timmy with milliseconds to spare. Was I indebted to Barner? There were those who would say so, yes.

I said, "Lyle, I really don't know how helpful I can be. It's hard to imagine that these neo-FFFers have any connection with the old FFF. The bunch that operated back in the sixties and seventies were ideological, but they were also hardheaded realists with attainable goals. Mostly rescuing the wrongly imprisoned from private mental institutions. This new gang is flaky as hell. Using intimidation to rid the airwaves of homophobia? It's a sweet impulse, but apparently these people are not familiar with the statutes on assault, or on extortion—or with the United States Constitution. Or with the realities of the American marketplace, either."

"They appear to be different people, that's true," Barner said. "But it can't be coincidence that they're calling themselves the Forces of Free Faggotry."

"They could have read about the old FFF. It's written about in some of the histories of the movement. Have you tried tracking down any of the old FFFers on your own? All you have to do is go into a bookstore or public library, find a good history of the modern gay movement, check the index for the FFF, get some names of people, and then locate them through your usual Orwellian technological means."

Barner's face tightened. "Yeah, I could have done that," he said. "I could even have figured out on my own that I could have done that. But I didn't do that."

"I see."

"Why didn't I do it that way? Why have I used the more roundabout method of bringing you into the case to track down the FFF?"

"Right. Why?"

"Because," Barner said, "I thought it would be nice to reconnect with you. That's one reason."

"Uh-huh."

"The other reason is," Barner said, his color rising again, "I don't go into gay bookstores. I don't go anywhere near the gay section in Barnes and Noble. I don't go anywhere near the gay sections in libraries. Get the picture?"

"Lyle, this is worse than I thought."

"I'm fucked up. I know."

"Are you out with Dave? Have you confessed to your boyfriend that you're a homosexual?"

Barner laughed ruefully. "Anyway, he can tell."

"Why didn't you ask Dave to help you find a book with the FFF in it? He sounds like the kind of man who might stride into a bookshop and brazenly make a purchase. Pat Buchanan's worst nightmare for America come true."

"I could have asked Dave for help," Barner said. "But to tell you the truth, I just didn't feel like getting something started."

"Right. So you arranged for me to drag my ass a hundred and fifty miles down the Hudson Valley, at the J-Bird's expense, just because you preferred not to have an argument with your boyfriend?"

"No, it's not just that."

"What else is it?"

"You'll be able to talk to the FFF people. They'll trust you. Even if they aren't the same people as back in the seventies and they don't know you from David Dinkins, you'll know how to get them to talk to you. They won't trust me, and they won't talk to me, because I'm a cop."

"This is possible."

"And like I said, the other reason I wanted to bring you into this was, I wanted to see you again. For one thing, I wanted to find out if you were the same smug pain in the ass you were sixteen years ago."

"And was I?"

"You're worse," Barner said. "I'm almost sorry I even mentioned your name to the J-Bird and his people."

"Almost sorry, but not quite?"

"You got it."

"Jeez, Lyle. What else is new? The more things change with you and me, the more they stay the same."

He watched me, poker-faced. He apparently was taking as much satisfaction from the love-hate—or to put it more precisely, like-dislike—games we were playing as he had when we observed the same awkward rituals sixteen years earlier. He said, "Anyway, Strachey, you're gonna love these

FFFers once you smoke them out. They're obviously a bunch of punk anarchists, and deep in your heart, that's you. It wouldn't surprise me if you brought them in and then you joined up with them."

"Lyle, you've nailed me again. I'm both a control freak and an anarchist."

"Think about it," he said.

"And when the J-Bird puts the FFF on his show, I'll be right there on the radio with them, promoting all my inconsistent causes and tendencies. Strachey the radical Presbyterian with J-Bird the broadcast postmodernist."

Barner said, "Don't believe that crap about the J-Bird putting the FFF on the air. He'll never do it. He wants to get them in here, and then he'll hire some goons to beat the shit out of them. That's how postmodern Plankton is. Anyway, after the tear-gas attack there's no way these people can avoid being charged."

"They can't be charged if they choose to deny doing the tear-gas attack and there's no good forensic or other evidence tying them to it. Is there any?"

"Not yet."

"As for the J-Bird's putting them on the air, listen to his show sometime. What Jeris is telling me is plausible. Plankton respects aggressive, and he respects nasty. He gets these people into his studio, and nobody will change anybody's mind. But they'll all hit it off famously in their twisted way. I think these guys might mean what they say about putting the FFFers on the show. At least in that regard, I think the J-Bird can probably be trusted."

Looking skeptical, Barner was about to reply when the door to Jeris's office opened and the J-Bird stuck his head in. "Hey, you two gumshoes want to meet a real, live FFFer?"

"That's the plan," I said.

"Then get your wide-load butts out here. One just walked in the door."

CHAPTER 5

A lanky man in his mid-forties with wavy straw-colored hair, china blue eyes and big ears was standing just behind the J-Bird in the corridor. In scuffed work boots, a pale green loose-fitting T-shirt and jeans faded not by fashion technicians but from wear, the man was sunburned across his forehead and nose. My guess for the source of the sunburn was a rare weekend out of the city, maybe waterskiing at Lake Hopatcong. But as I shook the sizable rough hand of Thad Diefendorfer—Plankton casually mangled the name, and Diefendorfer just as casually corrected him—there was a pleasantly rural aroma about Diefendorfer that suggested not outdoor sport but an outdoor occupation.

Diefendorfer confirmed this when he explained that he was a vegetable grower in central New Jersey. He had hauled a truckload of eggplants into the city, and while he was unloading at his wholesaler's Hunts Point dock he overheard a report on an all-news radio station of the tear-gas attack on the J-Bird and his crew.

"You weren't listening to the show this morning?" J-Bird said. "I find that hard to believe. Are you some kind of NPR elitist fruitcake, or what?"

Apparently uninterested in being provoked by Plankton, Diefendorfer said evenly, "I listen to public radio sometimes. I mostly listen to the all-jazz station in Hoboken when I can pick it up. I've never actually tuned into your program, Mr. Plankton. Maybe I should. What's it about?"

"What's it about?" Plankton sniffed. "What kind of a freakin' question is that?"

"Mr. Plankton's show," I told Diefendorfer, "is about Mr. Plankton. Now that you've met him, you can tune in weekday mornings from seven to ten if you want more of him."

We had all moved back into Jeris's office, where Barner said, "Thad, what made you come over here this morning? You're a member of the FFF that did the tear-gas attack?"

"No," Diefendorfer said, "I have no connection with whoever threw the tear gas, and I have no idea who they are. But if they call themselves the Forces of Free Faggotry, I just want to make it plain that they're not the original FFF. I was a member of that organization, and we were totally nonviolent."

"Sounds like a bunch of wimps," Plankton said.

"Why? Because we didn't want anybody to get hurt during one of our operations?"

"Well, no. You know what I mean."

"No, I don't. What do you mean?"

"I mean . . . I guess to somebody like you I have to stop everything and explain the obvious. I mean, if some mean bastard deserves a fat lip and you don't give him one, then you're a wimp."

Diefendorfer remained serene. He said, "So?"

"Whaddaya mean, 'So'?"

"So we're wimps. So what?"

"What do you mean, so you're wimps, so what? If you're wimps, you're . . . you're wimps. Do you *want* to be a wimp?"

"I don't care," Diefendorfer said mildly.

"Are you totally spineless?" Plankton asked, looking incredulous.

"No, not at all," Diefendorfer said. "I'm Amish."

We all looked at Diefendorfer. Apparently this was the last thing anyone in the room expected to hear.

After a moment, Plankton said, "You're shittin' me."

"No, sir."

Barner said, "And you're gay? You're gay, and you're Amish, and you're out of the closet?"

"It's actually more complicated than that," Diefendorfer said. "But basically, yes, I'm Amish, I'm gay, and I'm out. I'm also shunned in Ephrata, Pennsylvania. But I live in New Jersey, which puts up with me pretty well."

Plankton said, "But you're not wearing that black-and-blue getup that the Amish wear."

"No, not anymore," Diefendorfer said.

"Did you drive your horse and buggy up six flights?" Plankton asked. "I hope to hell you didn't ride up on the elevator. Wouldn't that be a heinous sin? Apparently, getting corn-holed is no longer a big deal among the Amish—which is news to me. It's not the Amish of—what was that Harrison Ford movie? *Eyewitness News* or something? But can you ride elevators, too? I seem to be behind the times."

"My horse and rig are out in the lobby," Diefendorfer told the J-Bird. "I walked up the stairs, but my horse, who's a Methodist, road up ahead of me."

"An Amish wiseass," Plankton sneered. "Now I've seen it all."

"And, homosexuality is still frowned upon among the

traditional Amish," Diefendorfer went on. "But personal conscience has always been respected among the brethren, and my conscience has led me farther afield than has been the case with some others. It's what led me to the Forces of Free Faggotry when I was eighteen, and it's why I came over here before I headed back to the farm. I came to tell you that the FFF was as righteous a community of men and women as I've ever known, and no true FFFer would ever attack anybody with tear gas. Not even anybody as confused and obnoxious as you are, Mr. Plankton."

Over the shades came a discernible movement of Plankton's left eyebrow. "You can call me J-Bird. There's no need to stand on ceremony."

"Okay. No true FFFer would ever attack anybody with tear gas. Not even anybody as confused and obnoxious as you are, J-Bird."

I had known Plankton for less than an hour, but I was not surprised to hear him ask, "Ever done any radio, Thad?"

"No, and don't plan to."

"You've got a smart mouth."

"I've been told that. I'm not proud of it."

"That's too bad."

I said, "The J-Bird wants you on his show, Thad, before the competition—WOR or WABC—discovers you."

"Strachey gets the picture," Plankton said. "ABC-Disney would know just how to market you too. *The Sarcastic Anabaptist* or some crap like that."

Barner, who unlike the rest of us was at this moment working for a living, said, "Thad, I'd like to hear more about your membership in the FFF. When did you say that was?"

"It was from May 1973 to February 1975. I can tell you about it if you like. Although, since you're law enforcement, you could easily look it up in my FBI file. I wouldn't mind having a look myself, if you get hold of it. When I filed a Freedom of Information Act request several years ago and the FBI finally mailed me a copy of my file, most of it had been blacked out."

Plankton whistled and said, "Christ, this is great stuff!"

I told Barner, "Lyle, you're saved. Why didn't we think of this before? You won't have to be caught entering a bookstore. All you need to know is available electronically."

Barner ignored this and said, "I'll see what the bureau has on the FFF."

"Was J. Edgar Hoover a secret member of the FFF?" Plankton asked. "That's probably the part they blacked out in your files, Thad. The stuff about Hoover and his boyfriend there—what was his name? Clyde Barrow?"

"Clyde Tolson," Diefendorfer said. "Right. J. Edgar and Clyde were both FFF moles in the FBI. His antigay hysteria was cover. Ingenious, wasn't it?"

Plankton laughed and shook his head. "Thad, you're breaking my heart, you know. You going head-to-head with Leo would be sensational, just sensational."

"Who is Leo?" Diefendorfer asked.

"He's on my show."

I said, "Leo Moyle is the J-Bird's resident racist–slash–fag-baiter. Next to him, the J-Bird is the show's Arthur Rimbaud."

"I liked those flicks with Sly Stallone gunning down commies," Plankton said. "So I'll take that as a compliment."

I said, "Thad, could you hang around in the city long enough for lunch? I'd like to hear your FFF story without a lot of kibitzing from the J-Bird, whose motives in this investigation are mixed, at best."

"You bet they are," Plankton said. "Though let me remind you, Strachey, that foremost among my motives is preventing any physical harm coming to myself and my staff. If you're going to take my money, it would behoove you to keep that in mind."

"I stand behooved on that point."

"Your employment is conditional anyway. We brought

you in because of your so-called contacts with the old FFF, and now along comes this old FFFer who says none of his people are involved in this thing at all."

"I don't guarantee that," Diefendorfer put in, "but I doubt it. Unless one of us has changed an awful lot over the years. There were sixteen people in the organization at one point."

Barner said, "This case has A-one top priority in the department. Although, of course, we want to be able to exploit all possible resources. So your retaining Don would be a real asset to the investigation, Jay."

"Glad to hear it. Maybe NYPD would like to pay him, too."

"Unfortunately, we can't do that."

Plankton found another can of Sprite in Jeris's office refrigerator and popped the tab. He said to me, "We'll bring you on for a week and see what you come up with. I'm not crazy about having a known homosexual on our payroll, and Leo is gonna be reaming my ass unmercifully over this."

"Ouch," I said.

"Unlike NYPD, which has to put up with a lot of political correctness, affirmative-action crap—six walleyed lesbians in every precinct house or whatever—I can hire and fire as I please, based on merit."

"I'll try to be meritorious," I said.

The J-Bird had his shades on, so he didn't see Barner blush when he looked at Plankton and said, "Some of the department's best officers are gay. If they're promoted, it's because they're effective, not because they're gay."

"God almighty, how naive can a man be? Where are you from, Detective Barner? Podunk? Mars? Albany? Whoops. I forgot. You are from Albany. Or at least spent one too many years up there in the little state capital that time forgot. What'd Ed Koch say that got him in hot water in the guber-natorial race with Cuomo? He wasn't sure he could stand being governor of New York, because there were no good Chinese restaurants in Albany."

Albany native Barner was spared having to reply truthfully, for at this point Diefendorfer cut in and said, "What's your hometown, Jay?"

"Experience," Plankton shot back. "My hometown is Experience in the World. I guess that's not a set of origins anybody'll ever be able to accuse you of, is it, Thad?"

"A big mistake people often make about the Amish," Diefendorfer said, "is assuming we're any less complicated than other people, or that our communities are any less familiar with the gamut of basic human experience. Anyway, since I've been 'living with the English'—that's what the Amish call it when someone leaves the community— well, since I've been out in the larger world for the past twenty-seven years, I'd venture to estimate that my experience has been at least as broad and varied as yours, Jay-Bird. And, based on my admittedly brief initial impression of you, twice as instructive."

Plankton laughed, and then he launched into another plea for Diefendorfer to come on his show and tangle with the J-Bird's sour, mean, white, straight, male chauvinist, Leo Moyle.

Even without Diefendorfer's unwillingness to join Plankton's drive-by shooting of a morning talk show, the chances that the New Jersey vegetable farmer would converse with Moyle any time soon plummeted when the door was flung open and Jeris burst into the room. Pale and bug-eyed, Jeris croaked out, "It's Leo! Leo's been kidnapped!"

CHAPTER 6

Half an hour later, I was on the phone with Timothy Callahan informing him that I would not be back in Albany until
late evening. I gave him a rundown on the series of alpha-
betized pranks played by the FFF on Jay Plankton, and
said, "It turns out that the *H* joke is no joke at all—not that
the earlier ones were all that funny. But this one is far more
serious even than the tear-gas attack. Leo Moyle has been
grabbed and taken away by somebody, who phoned the
radio station and said to tell the J-Bird that '*H* is for
hostage.'"

"Isn't that a Sue Grafton title?" Timmy said. "Or is the
H one 'homicide'?"

"I'm not sure," I said. "It's certainly not an E. Lynn
Harris title."

"I understand that. It's not an Alfred Lord Tennyson title, either. I thought maybe some of the FFFers were Grafton fans, and you could use that detail as an identifying characteristic."

I said, "Incidentally, who wrote 'The Oblong Box'? It's a writer whose name has only three letters in it."

"Is this another one of the FFF's clues?"

"No, it's another one of Will Shortz's. It's in today's *Times* crossword puzzle."

"Poe," Timmy said without having to think about it. "The oblong box was a coffin containing the corpse of a man's young wife. When the ship carrying it went down in a storm, the husband chose to forgo a seat in a lifeboat and stayed with his beloved's remains as they sank beneath the briny. It's a short story I read in high school."

"Had it been your body in that box," I said, "I'd have made for shore and returned on a sunny day with a nice wreath."

"Likewise in your case," Timmy said. "And I'd have brought along a six-pack of Molson tied to a brick."

"What about a three-letter word meaning 'spawn'? It's not 'kid,' is it?"

"It's probably 'roe,'" he said. "Does that fit?"

"I don't have the paper in front of me, but I hope to be back to it on the 8:10 train, which gets in at 10:30. I'll head straight home, though I'll probably be back down here tomorrow and stay for a few days." I explained to Timmy that while I found Jay Plankton and company repellent in all ways, I had agreed to sign on with them for five days at an inflated fee, partly out of morbid curiosity, even more out of economic self-interest, but mainly as a favor to Lyle Barner, who had once saved my life.

"Does Lyle still have the hots for you?" Timmy asked. "And did he remember me fondly?"

"He referred to you as 'that Irish kid,' so he obviously remembers you as adorable."

"What a strong, clear memory Lyle has."

"Or he may be confusing you with the young Mickey Rooney."

"If not the old Andy Rooney."

"Lyle's involved with a young cop, Dave-something. Dave is out in the department and Lyle's not, so there are problems. We're meeting Dave later, and also a former FFFer who turned up to deny involvement in the crimes and to vouch for the old FFF gang. This guy, Thad Diefendorfer, says they never did protests, just rescues, and always nonviolently. And Diefendorfer should know something about nonviolence—he's Amish."

Instead of blurting out, "He's Amish and *gay?*" as I would have, Timothy Callahan, being Timothy Callahan, said, "I've heard about homosexuality among the Amish. It's especially hard. I take it this guy has left his community."

"Years ago. He grows eggplants in New Jersey."

"Of course," Timmy said, "anybody who was in the old FFF gang would probably have the skills to pull off a kidnapping. That's essentially what the FFFers did: kidnap young people from secure mental institutions and hide them from their parents and the authorities. Are you sure you can trust this Diefendorfer?"

I thought about this, for the first time, really. "I think so. He comes across as genuine. I like him," I said, as it sank in that I needed to get to know Diefendorfer better.

"How was Moyle kidnapped? Right out of the radio station?"

"No, he'd left to meet a date for coffee at a Starbucks, and then never showed up. The date called the station to try to track Moyle down, and five minutes later a call came in from someone saying he was with the FFF, and they had Leo, and *H* was for hostage, and further instructions would follow. I'm at the radio station, and no more word has come in, but Moyle is definitely nowhere to be found."

"Maybe it is the old FFF," Timmy said, "and they're

going to put Leo in a mental institution—and try to turn the homophobe gay. Maybe do a poetic-justice job on him like the one in the Paul Haig case you worked on, where renegades from Vernon Crockwell's homosexual-cure psychotherapy group turned on the evil doctor and gave him a kind of dose of his own medicine."

I briefly thought that one over, too, and said, "Timothy, where are you dredging this wild stuff up from?"

"Experience, Donald. Yours, not mine, I should add."

"None of that is totally implausible. It's just that . . . a simpler set of circumstances is far likelier. You haven't seen the notes these neo-FFFers sent Plankton. They are not the work of sophisticated minds. These people are both crude and borderline loony. So far, I'd say a thoroughly nonbyzantine scenario is unfolding. My guess is, word will come from the kidnappers making some weird demand in exchange for Moyle's release. Maybe a demand that Plankton apologize to the homosexuals of America on his show—and then serialize a radio dramatization of *The Lord Won't Mind*. Anyway, it probably won't be long before we know."

"I hope you're right, but the whole thing sounds to me fraught with more complex possibilities. Maybe it's all being staged by Plankton and his people. How about that? A publicity scam. Have Plankton's ratings been going down? Has he been losing advertisers?"

"Not that I know of. Anyway, that'd be illegal. Staging a kidnapping, especially, would not go down well with the Manhattan DA's office. These people blather about 'edge' and 'pushing the envelope' and radio that's 'dangerous.' But just below the surface they're some of the most clunkily reactionary people in the country. They're Babbitts whose most profound interest is in their own comfort. They would never do anything that risked a big fine—possibly necessitating selling off a chunk of their General Electric stock—or, God help them, the quirky uncertainties of prison life.

For all their bravado, the J-Bird and his gang are not really risk takers."

Timmy said, "Oh, I don't know. They've hired you. For them, that's taking a chance. Of course, they may not know what they're in for."

"No, I've been up front with the J-Bird and his producer. They know I don't like them—even that I could turn on them."

"That's to their credit, then," Timmy said. "Unless, of course—and we're back to this—they brought you into this because they have something in mind that you're not aware of. Something . . . duplicitous."

"Timothy, you're making me a little nervous."

"Oh, Don, if I could only believe that," he said in his well-practiced way, "I'd be the happiest man in Albany."

I didn't laugh, just said, "Even beyond keeping me amused, you can be helpful in this."

"How?"

"Check my files on the Blount case and dig out the most recent address for Kurt Zinsser, the old FFF gay who harbored Billy Blount when he was on the run from his parents and the Albany cops. See if Blount himself is in the Albany area, and if you can't find him you might check those two women with the travel agency who were his buddies—Margarita something and Christine something. Christine was a fellow FFF rescuee. They may well have maintained contact with the old FFFers who, after all, saved their sanity and maybe their lives. They may know Thad Diefendorfer too—and he may know about them. I'll ask him. But anything you can do on that end to get the ball rolling, I'll be grateful for."

A little silence. He said, "You know, I'm at work."

"Sure, I know. But it's July. The entire legislature of the state of New York is in repose, on greens and fairways from Montauk to Jamestown. Who are you trying to kid, Calla-

han? And all of you legislative staffers in Albany are crank-
ing up the air-conditioning, kicking back in your bosses'
leather club chairs, and reading *Madame Bovary* aloud to
one another. It's summer at the capitol. I've been around
Albany as long as you have, and you can't fool me."

"You are largely mistaken, Donald," he said.

"Uh-huh."

"But when I get home from work at 5:18 P.M., I'll check
your files, make some calls, and see what I can do."

"Thank you, Timothy."

"See you around eleven, then?"

"Unless I join the neo-FFF myself and blow up the
J-Bird's radio transmitter, sure."

"You won't do that. You're no Babbitt, but you aren't
quite as adventurous as you once were, either."

I chose to take a wait-and-see attitude as to whether I
would regard Timmy's remark as a mere accurate analysis or
as a challenge.

CHAPTER 7

Barner was at the radio station questioning Leo Moyle's would-be date, a telemarketing supervisor named Jan Hammond, and Diefendorfer and I were seated in a booth at an inadequately air-conditioned garment-district coffee shop, where Barner planned on meeting us for lunch—if he had time for lunch, which, he said, he rarely did. Diefendorfer was telling me how he had heard about the FFF in 1973 and joined up with the group after his seventeen-year-old boyfriend, Ronnie Busby, in Ephrata, Pennsylvania, had been locked away in a Philadelphia mental hospital by his parents.

"When word got around about Ronnie and me, I was treated shabbily enough," Diefendorfer said, "but at least I had my freedom. I had already planned on leaving the community, so the shunning was tolerable. My mother and father didn't shun me, hurt and baffled as they were, and only one of my three brothers turned his back whenever I entered a room. But Ronnie just disappeared one day, and it wasn't until a week later that his eleven-year-old sister Beth told me what his family had done with Ronnie."

"Were you both still in high school?" I asked.

"Ronnie was a senior. I was homeschooled. My family were all house Amish, the most conservative branch. Ronnie was going to go to Millersville State College the following fall, and I was going to live with him, work, get my GED, and then go to Millersville, too—even though I wasn't sure why, besides being with Ronnie, I wanted to go to college. I did have some vague idea that I wanted to be an agronomist maybe, or a jazz saxophonist. When I was eight or nine, I heard a John Coltrane piece coming from the radio in a parked car at the Ephrata Agway—it wasn't until years later that I understood who and what I had heard—and I thought, someday I want to be able to make that sound. That urge stayed with me right up until the sad day I discovered that I have no musical talent whatsoever."

"Thad, this all sounds pretty gutsy for the early seventies. Especially an Amish kid being out. It was tough enough back then for the Methodists and Congregationalists."

Diefendorfer considered this. "I guess it was, but at the time I didn't think of myself as brave. During the year Ronnie and I were together—most of which time I most definitely was not out with anybody—I was torn between euphoria and sheer terror. When I was seventeen, a Dairy Queen went up near our farm, and my brother Emmanuel and I started hanging out there. That was pretty racy in itself for a Mennonite kid. It's where I met Ronnie when I was hanging around alone one Friday night having a shake. We kept looking at each other, and finally he came over and asked me if I was Amish—I had my farm clothes on—and he asked, were Amish people allowed to eat food made in a machine that ran on electricity?"

"That would have been my first question, too," I said.

"Well, the answer is no. But on an Amish sin scale of one to ten, ingesting a Dairy Queen product is probably only a one or two. The trouble was, however, that the more Ronnie and I talked, and the more that we looked at each other, the more I felt that a sin-scale ten was just around the corner for me."

"It was obvious that soon?"

"He invited me to go sit in his car with him. Which I did with no hesitation. I had been inside cars twice before, and I'd even ridden in one once. This alone made me a kind of Mennonite James Dean. Live fast—that is, go somewhere in a car—and die young. But when I climbed into Ronnie's dad's Pontiac that June night, it wasn't the car's internal combustion I was the most worried about, it was mine."

"You each guessed the other was gay?"

"Ronnie told me later he wasn't sure about me at first. Like most people, he naively believed that the Amish were somehow unlike the rest of the human race in that regard. But as soon as I got into the car with Ronnie and noticed that his hand was shaking, I was sure of what was happening, and I started sweating, and my hands started shaking too. I held up a palsied hand to Ronnie and said, 'Look.'" Diefendorfer raised a large, tanned, well-used hand above the table, as if to demonstrate. He made the hand tremble lightly, and I felt my own palms moistening and took a sip of iced tea.

"The only sex I'd ever had up until that time was with farm animals," Diefendorfer said, as casually as I might have mentioned carving polar bears out of Ivory soap when I was a Cub Scout. "But," he went on, "I'd been fantasizing about human beings—all guys—since I was nine or ten. And Ronnie was pretty close to my ideal: dark eyes, a mop of black curls, clear skin, reserved but not so shy that I had to worry he might panic and bolt. Anyway, when I showed him my trembling hand, he showed me his, and ten minutes later we were parked in a dark corner of my family's west pasture."

I said, "The male of the species is so efficient in these matters."

"It's our vestigial caveman genes. Spread that sperm around."

"And love followed close on the heels of lust?"

"Not close," Diefendorfer said, "but Ronnie and I liked each other immediately, and the sex was wonderful, and we kept finding ways to meet. Then, over the next year, as the time got closer for Ronnie to go away to college, we began to talk about our feelings for each other, and talking about how we felt made it even more intense and real. And the idea of actually separating for any length of time began to seem excruciating. Until, that is, it dawned on us that we didn't really *have* to separate. We were each an emotional and physical habit with the other that didn't really *have* to be broken, we realized."

"And all of this was kept secret from your friends and families?"

"Amazingly, yes. People found it a little peculiar that Ronnie and I were friends—he lived in town and went to Ephrata High, and I was house Amish out on a farm—but I was open about wanting to live with the English, so it was generally assumed that Ronnie was simply my modern-world guru. This was the case right up until Ronnie's Uncle Lloyd came over to borrow the Busbys' weed whacker one day while they were at an insurance agents' convention in Hershey, and he walked in on us while we were going at it in the Busbys' rec room. Then word spread fast, and a week later Ronnie was gone."

"His parents had him committed involuntarily? This

was legal in Pennsylvania? I know it was—maybe is—in too many jurisdictions."

"Ronnie was legally underage," Diefendorfer said. "His parents owned him. Legally, it was no different than if he had been a plow horse or a hog."

"It's hard to imagine that this medieval stuff has gone on in our lifetime."

"Well, it still goes on, I've read. Certainly in a lot of traditional societies. In the Middle East and parts of Asia and . . . where else? Alabama? Idaho? I know people here in the city who think the gay revolution is over. The legal fights that directly affect them have been pretty much won. Their main worry is that gay culture—whatever the term might mean to each of the wide variety of people who use it—is being diluted or is even disappearing. But for most gay people in most places west of Hoboken and east of Sweden, they might as well be living in 1951—if not 951. It's something I think about down on the farm. I've got a pretty good life now, but I know that an awful lot of people don't, and I'm not doing anything about it anymore."

"Do you go back to Ephrata?" I asked.

"Not often," Diefendorfer said evenly. "Last year my mother died. I wrote to the elders and requested permission to go to her funeral. They said no."

"They can do that?"

"I could have gone. They wouldn't have called the police. But . . . that's not the point."

"No."

"They complimented me on the righteous life I've led. They knew about my FFF exploits. Within the context of my being a sinner, I've been a man who helped others. They respected that and said so."

I said, "I guess it's a distinction Pat Robertson and his type of Christian don't take the trouble to make."

"That's right," Diefendorfer said. "It's why I still consider myself Amish. Through its history, the Mennonite faith has always had its dissenters. People breaking away and going off to found yet another branch. Mine is the Diefendorfer farm branch, I guess you could say. It has a membership of five."

"You and who else?"

"On the farm, it's my partner Isaac and me, plus Sarah Mintz and Esther Fenstamacher and their daughter Lizzie, who's three. Sarah is pregnant, and it'll be six of us in October. Isaac is Lizzie's biological father, and I'm the father of Sarah's baby—though only, so far, as a sperm donor through a clinic in New Brunswick. Sarah and I are the best of friends, though not lovers, praise the Lord."

"It sounds like a nice family," I said. "Though not, as the J-Bird pointed out, your classic, picturesque Amish household."

Diefendorfer laughed. "You don't know the half of it. We all met on—guess where? The Internet."

"I'm not surprised."

"There are Mennonites I know who've moved from the eighteenth century to the twenty-first in a matter of weeks. It's time travel, like science fiction. And I know some, too, who've visited the future—i.e., right now—and they've beat it right back to the less complicated past. Isaac and I— he's from Mifflinburg, Pennsylvania, and his history is a lot like mine—we try to combine those features of modern life we believe are morally neutral, like a Ford pickup, with the simplicity and cooperative spirit of traditional Amish life.

"It's hard sometimes. Isaac has never really dealt with his family's rejecting him, and he sometimes falls into black bouts of depression that last for days. And I get restless once in a while and yearn for my comical lost career as a jazz musician and my not-at-all-comical exciting youth, when I was the scourge of homophobes. But basically we like the lives we've made, and we manage pretty nicely. And since Sarah and Esther joined us three years ago, it's been even better—and easier, too, with the four of us working the farm. Financially, it's touch and go, but it helps that none of us are big consumers."

I said, "No twin Range Rovers parked side by side in the driveway of the Diefendorfer farmhouse?"

"No, but I have no objections to a beautifully made machine. It's one of the theological differences I had with the elders of my community in Ephrata. That and—as the J-Bird so eloquently put it—an appetite for corn-holery."

"Speaking of which," I said, "what became of Ronnie?"

Diefendorfer's sunburn seemed to intensify for an instant. He said, "Ronnie died. Years ago."

"Oh no."

"I did manage to get him sprung from the psych hospital his parents had put him in. When I found out where he was and tried to see him, they wouldn't let me in, naturally, or even let me talk to Ronnie on the phone, because I wasn't family. And, of course, because I was the coconspirator in ungodly activities and the alleged cause of what Ronnie's family called his mental breakdown. But I met some gay hippies in a park near where Ronnie was locked up in Philly, and one of them knew about the FFF and said this was exactly the type of cruel and unjust situation they specialized in.

"A week later, we had Ronnie out. As with most FFF rescues, we got help from sympathetic gay lower-level employees in the hospital. Ronnie was relieved and grateful, but neither one of us had a job or any money or even any marketable skills, really. Ronnie was a high-school kid who liked track and field, and I didn't know much more than how to drive a plow horse. It was all I could do to get on and off a subway train.

"We stayed with some of the Fairmount Park kids for a month or so. But Ronnie became more and more frustrated with the hand-to-mouth life and the overall uncertainty, and he told me one day that he was sorry but he was going back to Ephrata. He did go home, for a while, and lied to his parents that he had been cured of his homosexuality by the electroshock treatments at the hospital. I felt hurt and betrayed and lost, but I couldn't face going back to a place where a lot of people considered me an agent of Satan. I hooked up with the FFF, which was being financed by a rich stockbroker in Chicago whose parents had given him the treatment when he was a teenager, and I stayed with the group for almost two years. The FFF was righteous, it was a cooperative community, it was gay, and for me it was home. I was happy and fulfilled and free, for the most part.

"As soon as Ronnie hit eighteen, he left Ephrata for San Francisco, and I saw him a couple of times when some of us were doing rescues in California. By then, I was involved with Sammy Day, one of the FFF guys, and Ronnie was deep into the seventies San Francisco scene, with lots of happy-go-lucky screwing around. His timing was unlucky, though. When the plague hit, Ronnie went with the first wave. He was twenty-six when he died."

I said, "Those were the people who never knew what hit them. It didn't even have a name in the beginning."

"No, just things like 'gay cancer.' Most guys suspected, though, that it had something to do with all the fucking. That it was some kind of communicable disease. I saw Ronnie six months before he died, and he said, 'It sure was fun while it lasted.' That could have been me. I did a lot of casual screwing around, too. But I was moving around so much with the group that we tended to pair up, like some ancient Greek army of fuck-buddies."

"But in an age that had Edith Massey there to record it instead of Edith Hamilton," I said. Then I asked, "Did you know a man named Kurt Zinsser? He was involved in the rescue of two Albany kids around 1970 from a mental hospital in New Baltimore, New York. I met Zinsser briefly in seventy-nine when he sheltered one of the two kids,

Billy Blount, when Blount was being set up on a phony murder rap."

"Sure, I knew Kurt. He was still with the group in seventy-three when I joined up. He was a bit of a doctrinaire lefty, always quoting Fanon and Marx, and a bit tiresome in that regard. He stuck with the FFF after several of us got fed up and left in seventy-five."

"Any idea where he is now? In seventy-nine he was living in Denver."

"No, I've kept in touch with several of the old gang, but not Kurt."

"Thad," I said, "I certainly admire your going off and doing the Lord's work, so to speak, for the two years when you were with the FFF. But I'm wondering about one thing."

"What's that?"

"The first real skill you developed beyond eighteenth century–style farmwork was—there's really no more accurate way of phrasing it—kidnapping. That's what the FFF's work amounted to. True?"

Diefendorfer's big ears reddened now, and he laughed. "That's one way of putting it."

"So, I have to ask you. Let me just blurt it out. Have you had anything to do with the kidnapping of Leo Moyle?"

He grinned some more. "Nope."

"Your showing up to try to divert attention from the obvious suspects in the kidnapping, the old FFF, is certain to leave some investigators wondering. I'm sure Lyle Barner will consider the possibility of a cunning, elaborate plot."

"I'm clean," Diefendorfer said easily. "Anyway, I believe that I arrived on the scene *before* Mr. Moyle was abducted, no?"

"Well, before anybody at the radio station *knew* about the kidnapping, yes. But of course you could have known all about it, and timed your arrival to sow doubt and confusion just as the investigation turned urgent. Not so?"

"Strachey," Diefendorfer said, looking pleased, "you know, you're really getting my blood racing."

"Thank you. Please elaborate."

"Look, I left the FFF after two years because, as with so many radical organizations, things got complicated and even ugly after a while. Disagreements developed over philosophy and even strategy, and I could deal with that. Mennonites know how to find consensus. What I couldn't stand was the intrigue and backstabbing that got started after some new people came into the group. I came out of a background where people disagreed openly and resolved disputes in a mutually respectful way. The FFF conducted itself that way in the beginning, and that was one of the things I loved about it. The Forces of Free Faggotry was in a lot of ways Amish.

"But when the scheming got started, I was too naive and inexperienced in the world—and too shocked, really—to put up with the machinations, and I got out. I lived in a commune in Oregon for a while, and then ran a truck farm with some friends. I gradually adapted to the customs of life among the English, a lot of which I find reasonable and humane.

"But I'll tell you, Strachey, I really loved the excitement of those early FFF days before things went sour. It was a righteous life, and it was thrilling. So, when you talk about me being part of a kidnapping, it brings that all back. It gives me goose bumps just thinking about it. See?" Diefendorfer displayed a muscular forearm, and in fact the skin on it resembled the skin of a particularly masculine and well-shaped naked goose. This gesture was in keeping with Diefendorfer's apparent longtime habit of expressing his emotions with varying presentations of his limbs.

"I can see that you're feeling happily nostalgic," I said.

"I am, but that's all it is," Diefendorfer said. "Just nostalgia. The people the FFF snatched away wanted to be kidnapped. None of us would have carried off people who didn't want to be freed. Robbing people of their freedom, which is what someone has done to Leo Moyle, is the opposite of what we did. Being held against your will is a terrible thing. Some of the stories I heard from the kids we rescued would break your heart."

"But," I said, "don't you feel just a twinge of empathy—sympathy even—for the neo-FFFers, whoever they are, when they try to rid the public airwaves of a man who embodies the hateful impulse that got all those innocent young men and women you rescued locked up and tortured in the first place?"

"Sure, I sympathize," Diefendorfer said. "But, at the risk of sounding not righteous but self-righteous, I'll say that I also know that to fight evil with evil is to increase the amount of evil in the world. Usually. There may be exceptions, I know."

This sounded familiar. "Thad," I said, "I hope you can meet my cohort, lover and helpmeet Timothy Callahan. Your theology and his are similar. You two would hit it off. My own moral philosophy is somewhat more . . . English, you might say. Middle Eastern, even."

"I see."

"But if you sympathize even a little with the neo-FFF, as I do, just a tiny bit, you might be interested in a short-term project that just occurred to me."

He perked up again. "What's that?"

"You help me locate Leo Moyle and rescue him."

"Oh, I don't know."

"And if we could get to Moyle before the cops do, we could do the rescue in the name of the old FFF—redeeming your group's good name—and maybe even keep the neo-FFFers from going to Leavenworth. Unless we decided they deserved a lengthy incarceration, of course. Which they might."

"Hmm. Oh boy. Hmm."

"The other reason not to mention to Lyle Barner that we're working on this together is that he's gay and he is sexually jealous. He can't help it. It's something between him and me that goes way back. There's a history. It would drive him crazy if he brought me into this for his own not-entirely-healthy personal reasons and then I worked closely with you instead. But I think you can be more useful in the rescue than Lyle can, even if it turns out there is no connection between the old and new FFF, as you believe—but which, by the way, I'm not so sure of. It sounds as if your group had some people in it capable of considerable middle-age mischief."

Diefendorfer peered at me for a long moment, and then said, "Is this some kind of setup?"

"No, I'm not that clever, or Machiavellian."

"Well, I don't know about that."

"So, what do you say? How about one last heist?"

"But I have other responsibilities. To a number of people, and to thirty-five acres of eggplants, squash and beans."

"I guess that's true," I said. "I'm overlooking the obvious. Farmers don't have extra time on their hands for living out the adventure fantasies of the middle-aged."

Diefendorfer suddenly brightened. "But I suppose I could hire someone to do my deliveries for two or three days," he said. "There's a Princeton grad student who likes an occasional break from his dissertation research. He's worked for us before on short notice. Maybe I'll check and see if I can be freed up for a couple of days. It's possible, if we hurry this up."

"That's exactly the way the J-Bird and his people—and especially Leo Moyle, I'm sure—want us to work. Fast."

Diefendorfer smiled and said, "Would you look at that?" He showed me his goose-bumped right arm, and the hand at the end of it was trembling just perceptibly.

CHAPTER 8

"You and Thad have got something going," Barner said, as soon as Diefendorfer got up and went to the coffee-shop men's room. "I've got a sixth sense for these things. It's obvious to me that the two of you are way hot to trot. The sexual undercurrents at this table all during lunch were totally amazing, and I was definitely not included in the orgy. You planning on scoring a little Amish booty, Strachey? So, what's with you and the Irish kid back in Albany? It's an open relationship, or you just go ahead and fool around on the side, or what? Farmer Thad doesn't seem all that married, either, what with the looks being passed back and forth at this table for the past twenty-five minutes. It was really quite a sight to behold. I have to admit, I'm completely turned on by it."

Barner had arrived for lunch, sweating and checking his watch, half an hour earlier. He had informed us that a note signed by the FFF had been delivered to the radio station via bicycle messenger. Typed on a word processor, the note said Leo Moyle was alive and safe, and he would be freed at an unspecified later date, following his stay at an FFF "reeducation farm." No mention of a ransom was made, nor any release through negotiations.

Police investigators had quickly checked the messenger agency, whose dispatcher informed them that the note had been sent by a man in a New York police officer's uniform, and the delivery was paid for in cash. The dispatcher added that he suspected the sender was not a real cop, for instead of an engraving of the New York City seal on his badge, it had a picture of Cher.

Since no negotiations with the kidnappers seemed possible at this point, the police decided—with the concurrence of the J-Bird and of Leo Moyle's nearest relative, a brother in Boston—to announce that Moyle had been abducted and to ask the public for information that could help the investigation. It was also announced that the kidnappers had identified themselves as the Forces of Free Faggotry, "a radical gay organization" that had been harassing Jay Plankton for the past month and a half.

I said to Barner—whose sixth sense, like most people's, was being influenced less by the electromagnetic forces entering his brain than by the electrochemical forces already inside it—"You're reading something into the pleasant, if rushed, luncheon that you and I and Thad just enjoyed that wasn't there, Lyle. I do find Thad appealing. It's true, there's something pleasing to me about a nice-looking, fair-haired, sunburned man who smells vaguely of eggplant and who grew up in a household lacking a Krups latte-maker. Thad represents a combination of innocence and worldliness that I find attractive in a man. But is there anything consciously sexual going on between us—anything as significant as 'looks being passed back and forth,' as you put it? No, Lyle, there isn't. Your intuitive powers have failed you, I'm afraid."

Since Barner had in fact picked up *something* genuine between Diefendorfer and me, this haughty lecture was unfair. But Barner would not—could not—have approved of Diefendorfer's and my extralegal, borderline-rogue operation to rescue Leo Moyle and reclaim the FFF's righteousness. So he was going to have to remain in the dark temporarily. Tactically, letting Barner believe that Diefendorfer and I were "way hot to trot" would have had its diversionary advantages. But it would also have left Barner in a state of agitated sexual jealousy at a time when he had work to concentrate on. He might even have gone to Jay Plankton in a snit and had me canned.

Barner said to me, "Either you're lying—an excellent possibility with you, Strachey—or Diefendorfer is coming on to you and you're too thick to see what's happening."

"I don't think so," I said confusingly, just as Diefendorfer returned from the men's room and sat down in our booth next to me.

"So, Thad," Barner said. "Are you heading back over to Jersey now?"

"Yeah, I gotta get the truck back."

"Well, thanks for your help." Diefendorfer had phoned his partner Isaac and come up with a list of some of the former FFFers' last known addresses and phone numbers. I was given a copy of the list too and had promised Barner I'd check out the East Coast people on it, and pass on to him the names of possible suspects in either the harassment, kidnapping or both.

"I'm glad to do what I can," Diefendorfer told Barner. "But I doubt any of the old movement people would kidnap anybody who didn't want to be kidnapped. I've given you the names with the hope and expectation that all of these people will be cleared of any involvement in violent anti–J-Bird activities."

"People can change," Barner said. "And sometimes people you think you can trust can't be trusted at all, it turns out." He looked at Diefendorfer, then at me, then back at Diefendorfer, who looked at Barner, then at me, then back at Barner.

I said, "Well, let's just find out who's got Leo Moyle and see to it that Moyle is turned loose, and then we can rewrite history if we have to."

"Sounds good to me," Diefendorfer said, getting up.

"Have a nice trip back to Jersey," Barner said. "If we need additional information about the FFF, we'll know where to reach you."

"Sure, anytime."

Outside the coffee shop, Barner drove off in the unmarked NYPD Ford he had left parked in a towaway zone, and Diefendorfer said to me, "I'm not crazy about bamboozling Detective Barner. He seems to be a little bit paranoid to begin with, and we're just feeding his paranoia."

"I'm not wild about this either, but rest assured that Lyle's paranoia is a bottomless pit. The two of us will never fill it up. It is not going to overflow dangerously."

"Also, intriguing against people who are basically on our side makes me queasy, too. I can do it for the larger cause, if that's what it takes. But doing it this way does remind me of the guys who came into the FFF in seventy-five and turned the organization into an ego and power trip for themselves. Not that those are our motives. But still. You have no idea what a nightmare that was, and the basket case it turned me into for months afterward. I'd always thought living with the English meant using laundry detergent and doing the twist. My previous experience with human treachery had been pretty much limited to some of the grislier stories in the Old Testament. Then Mel, Lawrence and Alberto came along."

"Who were these people, anyway?" I asked. "They don't seem to fit the definition of righteousness that would preclude their showing up at this late date to harass the J-Bird and kidnap Leo Moyle."

Diefendorfer said, "I don't think we need to worry about any of those guys at this late date. They're long gone from the movement and its aims. Lawrence Piller is a vice president at the Fox News Network. I saw in the *Times* recently that another of them, Alberto Truces, is a Bush campaign official in Florida. And Mel Stempfle is an orthodox Freudian psychoanalyst who was prosecuted with two of his analysands several years ago in an insider stock-trading scandal."

"No," I said, "none of them seem to be likely suspects in a kidnapping—or people who might send somebody farm manure in the mail. Their MOs sound marginally subtler."

Diefendorfer said, "Farm manure?"

I explained the series of harassing mailings that had been sent to Jay Plankton, including the "excrement for the execrable" package of what had just recently been determined to be llama droppings.

"No," Diefendorfer said, "this is not at all the FFF I knew. I'm more convinced than ever that it's someone else doing all this weird stuff."

"And I guess your group never sold the FFF name and logo to somebody else, like Pan Am did."

"No, and I can't think of anybody in the old group who might have turned into a llama rancher. They were basically urban people. I was the only farmer in the FFF. Of course, now some people raise llamas as pets. They're friendly and docile, and there are quite a few of them around. They're not nearly as exotic as they were twenty years ago. They're good pack animals for trekkers, and some people raise them for the wool. Checking out all the llama owners in the Northeast for the source of the llama-manure mailing might take some time, if that's part of your job. Our job, I guess I mean."

"The NYPD is on top of the llama-crap situation, Lyle says, so we may be spared that task. Which is fine with me. I once saw a llama spit in a man's face, and it was not pretty. It's what llamas do on those rare occasions when they get mad or they're startled. It makes the regurgitation scene in *The Exorcist* look like Swee'Pea dribbling his porridge."

"Swee'Pea," Diefendorfer said thoughtfully. "Is that Popeye's baby?"

"Well, yeah."

"I'm subliterate when it comes to cartoon characters in the movies or on TV. I've caught up a bit, but there are gaps."

"Popeye was a comic strip originally. You didn't have newspapers when you were growing up in Pennsylvania?"

"Not for reading. We kept a stack of the *Harrisburg Sunday Patriot News* in the outhouse for reasons other than information gathering. But it was too dark in there to read, anyway."

"Thad, yours is quite a story. It truly is."

"I know. As you heard, Jay Plankton wants me to tell my story on his radio show. But I can't stand the man and don't plan on having anything to do with him after we clear the FFF's good name. What I do plan to do is come up with better ways than kidnapping and mailing in llama shit to make the J-Bird's life as unpleasant as possible and interfere, if possible, with his professional success."

I said, "Sounds good to me."

CHAPTER 9

"Jesus freakin' Christ," the J-Bird bellowed, "they could be torturing Leo right this very minute! They could have him tied down, like Lawrence of Arabia, with some big Turk fucking him in the butt, giving him AIDS!"

"I wouldn't go that far," Jerry Jeris said reassuringly. "I mean, what self-respecting homosexual would want to fuck Leo?" Jeris glanced at me, apparently hoping I would note with approval his use of the word '*homosexual*' instead of '*fag*'.

After Diefendorfer had left for his farm, I returned to the radio station where I planned on placing phone calls to old FFFers on Diefendorfer's list. I hoped, too, through these contacts to expand the list to include all of the thirty or so men and women Diefendorfer thought had been members of the group over the nine years of the FFF's existence. Also, Barner had put in a request for the FBI file on the old FFF and hoped to have it later in the day.

My phone calls, of course, risked tipping off the kidnappers that someone was on their trail. But surveillance of all thirty of the old gang was impractical, and eliciting old FFFers' suspicions of former comrades they had reason to believe might have gone around the bend would be helpful, as would information on younger, perhaps admiring acquaintances believed capable of radical political mischief in the FFF's name. Absent any of us coming up with some original-FFF connections, the investigation would have to depend entirely on forensic evidence, of which there was not much so far.

"Do you think we should up the reward?" Plankton asked Jeris. "Leo is going to be pissed as hell if there are people out there ripping out his fingernails in a rage because we're only putting up five K."

Jeris drew on his cigar—the two of them were producing flame and noxious soot like a Slovakian steel mill—and he appeared to mull over the cost-benefit ratios involved. He said, "I don't think the station will raise the amount at this point in time. Anyway, it's not a ransom, it's a reward. Rewards traditionally are much lower, aren't they?"

"Yeah, aren't ransoms usually in the millions?"

"I think so. Like the Getty kid, or some CEO in South America."

Plankton said, "The Lindbergh baby was cheaper, but that was a long time ago."

"Right, you've gotta factor in inflation."

"What do you think, Strachey?" the J-Bird asked. "How about earning your keep here and advising us? NYPD said start with the five-grand reward and see what it shakes loose. But if Leo is out there somewhere hanging by his balls, he's probably not too interested in an incrementalist approach."

I said, "I think your instincts are sound. I'd offer a hundred K at least."

Jeris rolled his eyes. "Jesus, Glodt would love that."

"Who's Glodt?" I said.

Now they both rolled their eyes. Jeris said, "Steve Glodt owns the station and the syndicate that sells the show. Steve still has the first dollar he ever made."

"He keeps it rolled up inside the gold-plated anal suppository he walks around with stuck up his ass," Plankton said.

"That's so it's out of reach of that blond nail-parlor operator Steve keeps on the side in Oyster Bay."

"But just *barely* out of reach," the J-Bird said, cracking up.

I said, "But doesn't Steve Glodt make millions from the show? A hundred thousand sounds manageable for an entrepreneur as rich as Glodt must be."

"Glodt is richer than God, and he'll be even richer if he can pull off the deal he's negotiating to get the show simulcast on one of the cable sports networks," Plankton said. "A hundred K is basically pocket change for that miserable prick."

"And he could probably write the reward off," Jeris said. "I could check on that and mention it."

"What about Leo's agent?" Plankton asked. "Would Irene have to be brought in?"

"What? You mean to agree on a figure?"

"Sure, and would she take her fifteen percent off the top?" Plankton said, laughing, and Jeris laughed, too.

"Glodt'd better get it right, or be prepared to take heat from Irene," Jeris said.

I asked, "Does Leo actually have a talent agent? The man has no talent."

Neither Plankton nor Jeris leapt to Moyle's defense. They just stared at me as if I were the dumbest thing they'd seen open its mouth in months.

"Strachey, do you have any idea what my show netted last year?" Plankton said.

"No."

"Try three-point-seven."

"Okay. Three-point-seven."

"The show's seven million listeners tune in for my refreshing iconoclastic wisdom predominantly, but they also tune in for Leo's fag and nigger jokes. Leo doesn't need talent. He's part of the rich chemistry of the show."

I said, "Maybe his agent shouldn't be called a talent agent. Maybe she should be called an asshole agent."

This got them haw-hawing again. There was no way you could insult these people. They knew how vile they were, and they adored themselves for it.

Plankton said, "There are TV news crews downstairs waiting to jump me when I leave the building. What if some bimbette from Channel 7 asks me how come we're nickel-and-diming Leo's emotional well-being, maybe even his cherry? I'll look hard-hearted and cheap."

"Refer them to Steve," Jeris said.

Plankton blew more smoke. "I don't suppose," he said, "that we could get one of Leo's ex-wives to go on camera and make a tearful plea to the kidnappers. They all hate him, don't they?"

"Yeah, but what about economic considerations?"

"I don't know what kind of deal he got from either Edie or Pam," Plankton said. "What about this gal he was hoping for a nooner with?"

"Jan something."

"How would she be on camera? The cops talked to her earlier."

"They didn't mention putting her out there," Jeris said.

Plankton grew reflective again. He said, "What about the mayor? Will he make a statement?"

"I doubt it'd help. Giuliani and these FFFers? No way."

"It'd be good for him politically to put in a nice word for Leo's virginity."

"Good and bad," Jeris said.

"Now that he's not running, he could give a fuck anyway."

Jeris brightened, and said, "What about Hillary?"

"What about her?"

"She's in bed with the gays. They think she's Shirley Bassey. Get her to plead for humane treatment of Leo and his release as soon as humanly possible."

Plankton looked doubtful. "Christ, after the vicious crap I've said about her and her husband? She'd go on Gabe Pressman and say too bad it wasn't me on the receiving end of the FFF's hot poker."

Jeris drew on his cigar. "And Lazio won't be any help."

"That dork, of course not."

"What about Archbishop Egan? The FFF knows he's just another antigay putz, but if he's out there pleading with the entire archdiocese to pray for Leo's safe return to his loved ones, it might rattle somebody's conscience who knows something."

The J-Bird shook his head. "O'Connor could have pulled it off, but Egan's too new. He's boxed in. Egan starts hotdogging and crashes, and it's back to the minors for him."

"Do they do that?"

"Not for tongue-kissing altar boys, but for political booboos, sure."

"Hey, wait a minute," Jeris said. "Doesn't Leo have a mother?"

"Yeah, but she won't be any help."

"Why?" Jeris said. "Is she black?"

The hilarity set off by that one went on for a good minute. After the laughter subsided, Plankton said, "Leo's ma's in a nursing home up near Boston, and she's down to her last marble. She's out of the equation."

The smoky silence in the room went on for a long moment. Then Plankton said, "I'd put up cash myself for more reward money, but, God, I'm paying off the boat, and—you know the rest of it."

Jeris snorted sympathetically. "I'm in a similar bind."

More rumination. Finally, Plankton said, "Either we call Steve in Center Island and put in a request for more reward money from the company, and by doing so incur Steve's wrath. Or, we count on the NYPD and our overpaid and so-far underutilized shamus here to save Leo's ass employing the meager resources at their disposal."

"I'm really sorry for you guys," I said. "What can you do? It's like *Sophie's Choice*."

At that, they har-de-hared, but a little tentatively, and then watched as I headed down the corridor to place my telephone calls.

CHAPTER 10

Julius, on West Tenth Street, had been a West Village tavern since the 1840s, when the Village was a village, and gay since the 1950s, a pre-Stonewall Mount Rushmore of Manhattan gay life. Washington, Jefferson, Lincoln and Teddy Roosevelt were three-deep at the bar when I arrived just before six to meet Lyle Barner and his boyfriend Dave Welch.

Barner had told me earlier on the phone that he had chosen Julius to meet in because it was friendly and it had good burgers. It would also be helpful for Dave to be reminded that not every homosexual in New York had been born last week, and that gay life could be about living comfortably in an unfair world and not pressing to change it twenty-four hours a day. It was also a bar, I knew, where hip neighborhood straights sometimes hung out. So Barner, anxious in all-gay venues, could retain the shred of closet-edness he seemed to require.

I half expected Welch to show up pierced and purple-haired, with the words QUEER BEER tattooed across his exposed buttocks, but when they came in together he resembled a younger version of Lyle Barner. Out of his patrolman's uniform, in Nikes, jeans and a blue-and-white striped polo shirt, Welch was thick and muscular, with a big head of bristly black hair that was only a little longer than his dark shadow of a beard. He smelled of precinct-house locker-room–shower soap, suggesting that he had just recently been naked, an additionally pleasing image.

Welch smiled at me slyly and said, "Lyle tells me you're assisting the department's detective division on the Moyle kidnapping. You're a fine citizen, Don."

"I'm just helping out in a small way," I said. "I once had a brief encounter with the Forces of Free Faggotry. Under the circumstances, that makes me one of North America's foremost experts on the FFF."

"Yeah, you and the Dutchman," Barner put in.

"I hope," Welch said, "that somebody can get to this Moyle asshole quick, because he's such a shit-for-brains homophobe that he might be too stupid to keep his mouth shut, and the FFFers could lose it and mess him up. My sympathies are with the FFF people, and I'd hate to see them all end up in Attica for the rest of their young lives."

"What makes you think they're young?" I asked.

"Their jokes, their language, their anger. I've done work with a gay youth group in Hempstead, out where I live on the Island, and some of these kids are very angry and very out of control. Lyle showed me copies of the notes the FFF sent to Jay Plankton, and I recognized the style—basi-cally, 'Mess with me and I'll hurt you or I'll hurt myself.' "

"I share your low opinion of Leo Moyle," I said, "and he's certainly a man who can incite rage. But the FFF people, young or old, strike me as more flaky than violent. So far, anyway, they've been more gonzo than vicious. More Hunter Thompson than Charles Manson."

"Kidnapping is itself violent," Welch said. "Anybody capable of inflicting that kind of terror is capable of inflicting any kind."

Barner had now snagged the bartender's eye, and we each ordered a draft.

I said, "The old FFF members were not only nonviolent, one of them was actually Amish, as Lyle is likely to have pointed out. So it does seem improbable that any of them are mixed up in this current anti–J-Bird mayhem. Though people sometimes do change over the years."

"The Amish guy sounds like a solid citizen," Welch said. "Though even there you can't put too much faith in a label."

Barner said, "There are even Amish heroin addicts now. There was a bust in Ohio a couple of years ago."

"Lyle, I examined Thad Diefendorfer's arm. I saw no needle tracks."

"Anyway," Barner said, watching me, "Diefendorfer is clean. I ran him, and I talked to the chief in Burns Ford, where he lives. The chief asked around, and he went over and checked out Diefendorfer's farm. There aren't any llamas, and no sign that Moyle might be being held there."

I gazed at Barner. "Was that necessary?"

"What?"

"Hassling these gay Amish. This decent man who showed up on his own to offer information."

"What information?" Barner said, trying to look irked. "A twenty-year-old list that we're supposed to go chasing after? Sure, something on the list could pan out. Or the list could be to throw us off. I don't know about you, Strachey, but in my experience every lead has to be followed. Even leads where I feel like getting in the suspect's pants but I'm too professional to do such a thing."

My guilt fell away like an old scab. Working ahead of and around Barner now felt not only like the fairest method for dealing with the FFF, but like the most effective way to proceed with the kidnapping investigation. Barner had obviously been addled into temporary incompetence by his jealousy. Scamming him also seemed to be exactly the duplicitous treatment that he had coming.

I said to Welch, "Lyle thinks I've got something going with Thad Diefendorfer, a man I met for the first time this morning. But he has misread the situation. I'm interested in Diefendorfer's political and organizational history, not his—"

I paused, and Welch cut in with, "Pale eyes, clear skin and sturdy outdoorsman's physique?"

"How did you know that?"

"Lyle told me," Welch said, and grinned. "Me, I don't have Lyle's training and experience. But any of these old FFFers sound like they need to be vetted, and Diefendorfer comes across as an excellent resource. Even if none of the old FFFers turn out to be good suspects, younger people who they know might be. I know a little bit about the movement—I've done some organizing with gay officers in the department—and I had never even heard of the FFF until they started yanking the J-Bird's chain."

"Dave, that's why I brought Strachey into it," Barner said. Our beers had been set on the bar, and Welch reached through the knot of men in after-work jackets and ties and handed the glasses out one by one.

Welch raised his glass to Lyle and said, "Credit where credit is due. I'm talking as if I knew a lot more about criminal investigations than the stuff I've learned from Lyle, but I don't. I've taken a few courses at Hofstra, but if I ever make detective, most of what will get me there I'll have gotten from Lyle, a good teacher and a good cop, and a good baby-that's-not-all." Welch winked at me, and Barner colored and looked pleased.

"Can you make detective if you're out in the department?" I asked. "Lyle says you've had kind of a rough time."

"Yeah, kind of," Welch said. "I've had human shit packed into my shoes. My locker's been painted pink. My service revolver was tossed in a laundry basket and a Jeff Stryker dildo stuffed in my holster in its place. Other hilarious pranks like that. I've filed formal complaints seventeen times, and every time I complain, the complaint is filed and I'm written up for causing morale problems in the precinct. So, can I make detective under these circumstances? Not under this mayor and commissioner, no. But things are improving a little bit at a time. I know there are a lot of gay cops in the department, and the more of them who come out and say they're not gonna put up with this shit, that helps."

Both of us were careful not to look at Barner, who was busy watching us being careful not to look at him.

It was Barner who said, "In a way, it really sucks that we're the ones trying to bail out the J-Bird's homophobic ass. The meanest clowns in the precinct are big J-Bird fans, and they've always got him and Moyle and those other morons on the squad-room radio in the morning."

"It's a fucking rotten way to start the workday," Welch said, and raised his beer glass. "Here's to Leo Moyle's reeducation at the hands of the FFF before his safe return to the New York airwaves." We drank to that.

Barner asked me how I'd made out tracking down old FFFers, and I told him truthfully that I hadn't come up with much yet. "I talked to one guy in Cleveland and two others in Los Angeles who had fond memories of their FFF days. They talked the way Timothy Callahan and his Peace Corps buddies carry on when they get together—the VFP, Veterans of Foreign Peace. Lots of stories from the sixties— oft told, I'd guess, with a sardonic warm glow and a certain amount of editing and refining.

"These old FFF guys had not heard of the kidnapping,

they said, and I believed them. They were unhappy—disgusted even—with the FFF name having been taken up by kidnappers. All three said they couldn't imagine any of the old gang doing such a thing, and none could think of any radical Gen Xers they knew who might adopt the name and carry out FFF kidnappings or tear-gas attacks."

I told Barner that I had not yet been able to reach most of the people on my FFF list—which one of the LA contacts had added two names to—but that I would keep slogging away, and even visit two former FFFers who were living in the Northeast, one in central New York state and one in Connecticut. Barner asked me about Kurt Zinsser, the FFFer I met in Denver in seventy-nine while working on the Blount case, and I said Zinsser apparently was no longer in Denver, and no one I had spoken to knew what had become of the old new-lefty.

"I've got something to tell you, and you're not going to like it," Barner said.

"Not like what?"

"I got hold of the FBI file on the FFF."

"That might help. What's not to like?"

"You're in it."

Welch said, "Hey, a man with an FBI file. You must be doing something right, Don. Unless you're in the KKK, NAMBLA or the Eagle Forum."

"What am I doing in the FFF's file? I know I've got an antiwar file, but FFF? Have you got a copy of it?"

"Back at the precinct," Lyle said. "It's not that you were FFF. It's about Kurt Zinsser and the Blount case. Zinsser and the FFF rescued Billy Blount from the funny farm his parents put him in when he was a kid, and later you rescued Blount from his parents when they tried to use the phony murder charge to have him committed a second time. Did you know that afterwards the senior Blounts tried to have you charged with obstruction of justice?"

"No."

"They did. Stuart Blount and his lawyer, Jay Tarbell."

"Tarbell. That slug. I ran into him on Washington Avenue last week. He came out of the Fort Orange Club, patted his new Mercedes 230 SL on the hood ornament, and winked at me."

Barner said, "In January 1980, the US attorney turned the case over to the FBI. The bureau looked at the thing, and the investigating agents concluded you had probably broken an undetermined number of laws in the course of clearing Billy Blount of the Steve Kleckner murder. But they weren't sure which laws they might have been. The assistant prosecutor in charge doubted his office could make obstruction of justice stick, so the top man decided to pass, in spite of pressure from Tarbell and Albany city hall."

"Bill Keck," I said. "A Jimmy Carter appointee who always struck me as a reasonable man. I never knew just how reasonable."

Welch was looking at me intently. He said, "Lyle described you as some kind of anarchist. A hippie without the incense and the love beads. But it sounds as if you knew exactly what you were doing, and you were nimble as hell."

Anarchist? Hippie? Were? "I've managed to right a few wrongs over the years in a borderline sort of way and still stay out of Leavenworth. I've also wronged a few rights, but we don't need to get into those."

Barner snorted and said, "I'll say."

"What else is in the FBI report on the FFF?" I asked. "I'd like to see it."

"Stop by the precinct and I'll make you a copy," Barner said. "But overall it's the same names Diefendorfer gave us, and not even as up-to-date. The file is fun to read, though. I wish I had the *cojones* to pull off some of the stunts the old FFF guys got away with."

We both looked at Welch, who I guessed we all knew had a similar wish for Barner. But Welch just said, "I'd like to read the report, too, but later. I've gotta be somewhere at eight-thirty."

Barner tensed, and I guessed I knew what that meant. While we had burgers, Barner told stories of some of the old FFF's more daring exploits as described in the FBI files, and then Welch departed. As I left with Barner for his office and then my train back to Albany, I asked Barner if Welch had a date with someone else.

"There are two of them," Barner said. "Dave asked me to come along, but I'm not into that. He's asked me several times, even though he knows that's not what I want in a relationship. They're constantly doing poppers and shit like that. The three of them also use other substances, Dave admitted to me one time, that no police officer should get anywhere near, personally speaking. This isn't for me, Strachey. I want Dave, I go for Dave, but this is not who I am."

I wondered if Barner had figured out that, since Welch repeatedly offered things that were repugnant to Barner, the offer was either a cruel taunt or perhaps not sincerely meant. Now I was feeling sorry for Barner and guilty all over again.

CHAPTER 11

Timmy said, "If you'd join the twenty-first century and carry a cellphone, I could have reached you."

"You could have located me through Lyle, through NYPD. I was with Lyle at a bar in the Village, and you could have had him paged. What you've come up with is terrifically important. Of course, it is better that Lyle not know about Zinsser just yet. I want to check this llama-farm thing out on my own first, along with Thad Diefendorfer."

"Right," Timmy said. "You and Thad, the Mennonite middle-aged caper artist. The Lavender Hill mob rises again."

We were seated on the glider out on our back deck under the summer stars, which were just barely visible through the blaze of Friday-night light from nearby Lark

Street, Albany's Via Veneto. Timmy had made some of his superb guacamole, a skill he had mastered, inexplicably, during his Peace Corps tour in India. He had also brought out a Molson for me, and for himself a chardonnay selected for its fluty tone and delightfully twee outlook, as well as for its reasonable cost at the Delaware Avenue Price Chopper.

I said, "When they decided to rob the Bank of England, the Lavender Hill mob were mostly over-the-hill has-beens, whereas I am an accomplished professional investigator at the peak of my powers. So the has-been description certainly doesn't apply to me."

"Of course not."

"And when you meet him, you'll see that while Thad's guerrilla-activity skills might be rusty from disuse, he's as keen and fit as ever."

"Fit and keen. Sounds good."

"Of course, I didn't know him way back when."

"Explain to me again," Timmy said, "why you're pairing up with Diefendorfer to work ahead of Barner and the police instead of with them. I still don't quite get that."

"Oh?"

"What it sounds like is, you've resumed your twenty-year-old head games with Lyle, where you two play out your sexual attraction to each other—which for practical and personality reasons is futile—with complex little rituals of mutual psychological abuse. I used to be the not-directly-involved third party in the ritual, but now it's Thad Diefendorfer. Having Diefendorfer involved instead of me adds an extra charge, because however uninterested you are in him on a conscious level, he sounds like he's just enough of a turn-on to get you radiating little testosteronal vibrations that Lyle picks up and which drive him up the wall.

"Which is what nature apparently intended for you and Lyle to do to each other now and unto eternity. Plus, of course, Diefendorfer *does* sound like an interesting guy to be around, so I'll envy you that. If, that is, you decide to proceed with this plan to free Leo Moyle on your own, ostensibly to save the neo-FFFers from their own wretched excesses. But I have to say that the whole thing sounds pretty wacky to me."

Almost from the moment we met, Timmy had a way of explaining me to me with such thoroughness and stark plausibility that it threatened to use up all the analytical oxygen in the room. It was one of the reasons I was in awe of him, and when he did it, it filled me with love and terror. My conflicting impulses were always to adore him unabashedly, or to get my revolver out of the bedroom closet and pump him full of hot lead.

I said, "There may be a certain amount of truth in what you say."

"Uh-huh."

"But one part you're leaving out is, Lyle is far more discombobulated by me than I am by him."

"I'll take your word for that."

"So my working closely alongside Lyle, as opposed to in approximate tandem with him, would actually hurt the investigation. Lyle going around unhinged would not be good for Leo Moyle, for Jay Plankton, or for Lyle himself."

"Surely not, no."

"And, as for Thad Diefendorfer's playing out recover-your-youth adventure fantasies—or, should you choose to think of such a thing as being my own motivation here, laughable as that diagnosis is—*if* either of us actually happened to be so motivated, so what? It's for a good cause, halting dangerous criminal activity. And, if we succeed, we'll be well-armed with both influence and knowledge in case we decide to chasten or just dilute the influence of the ghastly Jay Plankton—or even, if we can, ruin him for life."

"Well then," Timmy said, "it looks like you're going to do it. Whatever 'it' is."

"You bet."

"In for a penny, in for a pound."

"There comes your Georgetown education again."

"I'll wager you were exposed to similar thinking at Rutgers."

The starlight reflected off Timmy's pale Gaelic half-profile, which I never tired of viewing from different angles, and off his wineglass, which he raised in a salute to the inevitable, more dubious surprises from me.

I said, "I'm amazed you tracked down Kurt Zinsser so fast."

"It was easy. Billy Blount, though, is long gone from Albany. He works for the Bank of America's office in Singapore, where he's got a Chinese boyfriend. The senior Blounts are still here in Albany, but Billy has as little contact with them as he can get away with. I learned all this from Christine Porterfield, who still runs Here 'n' There 'n' Everywhere Travel with Margarita Mayes out at Stuyvesant Plaza. They visited Billy in Singapore last fall, where they celebrated the thirtieth anniversary of their rescue by Kurt Zinsser and the FFF."

I said, "The FFF has such a noble history, it really is a shame that the name has been tainted by—whoever."

"Billy, Chris and Margarita had not been in touch with Zinsser himself for many years," Timmy said. "But they knew where he was, because a friend of Chris's in the Berkshires got interested in llamas, visited Zinsser's farm last summer, and recognized the name. When the friend mentioned Chris and Billy to Zinsser, though, he cooled off, Chris said, and showed no interest in reestablishing contact. So the friend dropped the subject and stuck to discussing raising llamas."

"Where in the Berkshires is the farm?"

"Monterey, Mass. Zinsser has an operation of some local renown. He produces something called Berkshire Woolly Llama Cheese."

"Woolly cheese?"

"It has quite a reputation, Chris says. You can pick it up

at a number of health-food and New Age–type stores over here."

"There's wool in the cheese?"

"I wondered about that, too. It's a soft cheese, and apparently you suck it out of the wool. The oil in llama fur contains some kind of protein that's healthful in a variety of ways and is supposedly conducive to spiritual well-being. There are pre-Columbian Inca legends about woolly llama cheese, according to Zinsser's advertising, Chris says."

"Hmm."

"I know. A nice, ripe Camembert sounds more uplifting to me."

"So, up and down the Berkshires—from Tanglewood to Mass MoCA to the Norman Rockwell Museum—there are robust, spiritually improved people going around picking llama wool out of their teeth?"

"That's the report I received."

I said, "Then I think Zinsser is our man for sure—the harasser, sending Jay Plankton llama droppings and all the rest of it, and the kidnapper of Leo Moyle."

"Why are you so certain?" Timmy asked.

"Because he may once have been a mere radical gay liberationist, but now Zinsser sounds capable of just about anything. Woolly llama cheese? God."

"So, are you going to call the FBI? I probably don't have to remind you that transporting a kidnap victim across a state line is a federal crime."

"No," I said, finishing my Molson. "I still think it would be best for everyone concerned if I handled this myself. I'm going to call Thad. And since tomorrow is Saturday, maybe you could join us for a drive over to the scenic Berkshires."

Timmy looked doubtful. "Should I bring along a firearm?" he said.

"No, I'll handle that. You bring the toothpicks."

CHAPTER 12

Diefendorfer drove up from New Jersey in the morning, and by noon he and Timmy and I were on the road headed east. During the hour's drive over to Massachusetts, Thad told us stories of FFF rescues he had been involved in or had heard about from his cohorts. Most rescues, he said, were not especially difficult or dangerous; they involved winning over or just bribing lower-level mental hospital employees, many of whom were gay and often eager to be helpful. Doors were left unlocked, alarms disengaged or shorted out, escapees stashed in car trunks. Cash for bribes was always available in the FFF's later years as grateful young rescuees from wealthy families turned twenty-one and were not only immune to involuntary commitments but also gained access to their trust funds.

Rescues that could not be effectuated through these means were harder but also more exciting, Thad said. At one point a gay former cat burglar—rehabilitated after a stay in an Indiana penitentiary and retired from crime, he claimed—was brought in to teach a course in breaking and entering. Thad told us he had taken the course and was one of the foremost lock pickers in central New Jersey. Or had been; some locks worked electronically now, or were even computerized, and Diefendorfer had not kept up with the technology.

Timmy, educated by Jesuits, and Thad, the Mennonite second-story artist, had a good talk about Augustinian ideas of combating great evils by employing lesser evils if and when they became necessary. My own easygoing tendencies in these areas were well known to Timmy, who once described my companionship with moral relativism as "hair-raisingly blithe." He considered my late-adolescent departure from the Presbyterian Church "intellectually vacuous" mainly because it had turned Beethoven's and Schiller's "Ode to Joy" into an "Ode to Good Taste." So it was interesting to listen to these two chew over moral questions I had sometimes been forced to grapple with in my line of work, and to hear them come down, if not as close to Satan as Timmy sometimes thought I belonged, then closer than either one of them might have admitted if described in those terms.

Uncertain that we would want to make a meal of Berkshire Woolly Llama Cheese—Thad said, "I didn't come prepared to comb my lunch"—we stopped in Great Barrington at the Union Bar and Grill for salad and Cuban pork sandwiches. This inviting local landmark, with its metal sculptures and SoHo-in-the-hills brushed-aluminum interior, was packed with weekenders from the city. Some were in the Berkshires to have their souls filled up with art, theater, music and dance. Others, less transported by the offerings of the Boston Symphony Orchestra or the dancers at

Jacob's Pillow, at least were getting their cultural tickets punched.

After lunch, en route east over the hills on winding, woodsy Route 23, Timmy, Thad and I worked out a plan. The chances were good that even after an event-filled twenty years, Kurt Zinsser would recognize me. So rather than spook him, we decided Timmy and Thad would engage Zinsser and keep him occupied while I looked around the farm. Then I would move in for a confrontation based on what I did or didn't discover.

The Berkshire Woolly Llama Cheese Web site had provided us with directions and informed us that visitors to the farm were welcome. That made it less likely, we figured, that Leo Moyle was being held captive in the main farmhouse or cheese factory, but was probably somewhere nearby.

In the center of the village of Monterey, we turned down a country road just past the general store, where about half the cars parked out front had Massachusetts plates and the rest were Volvos and Saabs from New York and Connecticut. The narrow road followed a meandering brook through stands of maple, hickory and birch, and meadows where cows and sheep once had grazed.

Few of the farms were working now, however, and instead of John Deere and International Harvester machines outside the barns, there were sleek sedans from Germany and Sweden, and Detroit SUVs the size of Soviet troop carriers for hauling the peasant bread and radicchio out from Great Barrington. The white clapboard farmhouses were beautifully kept, and many of the barns, also bright white, were now garages or guest houses with skylights and discreetly placed satellite dishes.

We passed the farm that produces renowned Monterey *chevre*—in a pasture several goats frolicked for our amusement—and then we drove on for another mile or two until we spotted a herd of llamas in a field. Then came the farmhouse and a large, faded, red barn nearby, with a sign on a post that read: Berkshire Woolly Llama Cheese, the Spirit of the Ancient Incas in a New England Country Setting.

Diefendorfer said, "It's like Grandma Moses at Machu Picchu. It's a little confusing."

Timmy asked, "Didn't you get a lot of this kind of cultural fusion—or at least weird commercial exploitation—in Lancaster County? Chain-hotel cocktail lounges with Pennsylvania Dutch happy hours, and so on?"

"We did. One of my favorites was a hex-sign extermination service. I once heard about a brothel over in Bucks County where for eighty-five dollars a dominatrix in an Amish farmwife's garb would raise welts on customers' bare backs with a buggy whip. But I don't know if that story was true. Pennsylvania has never had much tolerance for commercialized sin. Historically, it's one reason New Jersey exists."

"Demand and supply," Timmy mused.

"Yes," Diefendorfer said, "the Bible should have included a book called Market Forces, with special verses commenting on New Jersey."

We pulled into the Berkshire Woolly Llama Cheese parking area and stopped under a big spreading oak. Bees buzzed and flies zigzagged through the thick air, and the place smelled of warm green growth. A sign directed visitors to the barn, so Timmy and Diefendorfer headed over there in search of Kurt Zinsser while I ambled over to the wire fence to look at the llamas. A mud-spattered Chevy Blazer with Massachusetts plates was parked next to the barn, and closer to the house was a newer, cleaner Chevy 4×4 pickup. There were just the two buildings, close to the road and not far from each other, and it now seemed to me unlikely that Leo Moyle would be held captive in so public a place. Traffic on this rural lane was light, but the location didn't feel isolated enough for the safety and security serious kidnappers would need.

I watched Timmy and Diefendorfer disappear into the visitors' entrance to the barn, then turned back toward the dozen or so llamas. The two nearest peered my way while the others continued to graze. With their big soft eyes and alert pointed ears, the llamas looked like friendly storybook animals, maybe from A. A. Milne. I half expected them to be holding toy buckets and shovels, or even to speak: "Pleasant day, amigo."

Unsure of what to do next—approaching the farmhouse made no sense—I was about to join Timmy and Diefendorfer in the barn, when the screen door to the farmhouse opened and a stout, middle-aged man clomped across the porch and down the steps. His head was shaved, and he wore jeans, work boots and a sweat-stained T-shirt. The shirt had a picture of a llama on the front, and the lower half of the animal, stretched across the man's ample belly, was distorted, as if the llama had been blown up like a balloon.

I didn't recognize him at first, but Kurt Zinsser looked my way and did a double take.

"Denver?" he said, coming over to me. "Nineteen—what? Seventy-nine? Eighty?"

"I'm not sure," I said, struggling to look blank. "I've only been to Denver once. It was around that time that I was there, as I recall. Wait a minute. You're not . . . uh . . . uh?"

"Kurt Zinsser. And you're a private investigator. Bill Straithwaite?"

"Don Strachey. I didn't recognize you at first. You had a big, bushy beard back then, like Alexander Pushkin or the Maharishi Mahesh Yogi."

Cordial enough and definitely curious at first, Zinsser now began to look suspicious. "What are you doing here? Are you looking for me?"

"No, I'm with some friends, just poking around the Berkshires. Is this your farm? Are you the Berkshire Woolly Llama Cheese tycoon?"

Zinsser glanced toward the barn, noted Timmy's

Honda, and said, "I'm on my way into Barrington. Sorry I can't show you around. But Darren's in the shop and he can help you out. Have you had our cheese?"

"Not yet. I'm looking forward to trying it. It's unusual."

"I learned to make it from an old woman I met in Cuzco. That's where I went after I left Denver in eighty-five. I heard it was going to be the high-tech center of the Andes, which turned out to be not quite true. But I found my health there, physical and spiritual."

"And your livelihood. I hear Berkshire Woolly Llama Cheese is catching on."

"You'll understand why once you've tried it. Eat it every day for a month and you'll be a different person."

Since Thad Diefendorfer was not present, I asked the question I knew he would ask. "Why would I want to be a different person?"

Zinsser smiled a smile that I guessed he thought of as enigmatic. He said, "If you have to ask, you may never find out. But read my chapbook—you can pick one up in the visitors' center—and perhaps then you'll begin to understand what I learned in the mountains. And if you choose not to open yourself up to the wholeness of being, it's no skin off my ass."

I said, "I heard Billy Blount has done some traveling, too. Someone in Albany told me recently that he's in Singapore. Are you two still in touch?"

I could see the lightbulb go on inside Zinsser's head, and he looked at me hard. "Are you part of the investigation?" he said.

"Which investigation?"

"The investigation of Leo Moyle's kidnapping."

"I might be."

Zinsser snorted. "What horseshit. What a lying sack of bull puke you are, Strachey. Good Christ Almighty!" Zinsser shook his head, which glistened with sweat in the afternoon sun. His more spiritual self was not in the ascendancy.

"Are you a Jay Plankton fan?" I asked.

"You're friggin' right I am."

"You talk like him."

"I'm flattered."

"Aren't you gay anymore? Have you become one of those ex-gays?"

"No, but I no longer parade myself around the American landscape wearing a big sign that says Victim. Instead of whining about how oppressed I am, I lead a life of dignified self-sufficiency."

"If you're a Plankton fan," I said, "you must have as much wool in your brain as you've got in your teeth. His loathing for you and me and other gay people is vast and unadulterated. Plankton could care less if you've turned into some kind of neoconservative twit. To him, to be gay is contemptible. And you still admire him?"

Zinsser, the former Marxist, SDSer, FFFer, et cetera, sniffed and said, "Plankton is not antigay; he is anti–politically correct. That's something the J-Bird and I very much have in common."

"Cut the crap, Zinsser. Eight times out of ten, people who use that term are bigots and creeps. Anti-PCism is the current last refuge of the incorrigibly narrow and mean-spirited. So, is the FFF just more political correctness run amok? Is that what it was when you were part of it in the seventies?"

"I am neither ashamed of nor embarrassed by my years in the FFF. But if that's why you're here—which appears to be the case—let me assure you I have had no association whatsoever with the Forces of Free Faggotry since 1977. And I know for a fact that the organization fell apart soon after I left it. These people who are hassling Plankton and who kidnapped Leo Moyle are *not* FFFers. I am certain of that because whatever we were, we were never violent and we were never childish."

I looked at him helplessly. This was not the Kurt

Zinsser I was hoping or expecting to find. After a moment, I said, "You've done quite a one-eighty over the last twenty years, Zinsser."

Looking smug, he said, "Oh, I have at that."

"Do you remember Thad Diefendorfer?"

"Sure, the Mennonite-farmboy-turned-cat-burglar. I once had a crush on him for about ten minutes. But he was joined at the hip at the time to Sammy Day, another member of the organization. Why do you ask?"

"He's over in the barn."

"Thad is? What's he doing here, with you?"

"We're looking for Leo Moyle. Thad wants to help clear the FFF's good name, and I'm working for . . . a client."

"Which client? Who is it?"

"My client prefers to retain his privacy."

Zinsser's eyes got bright. "It's Jay Plankton, isn't it? You're accepting the filthy lucre of this man you malign behind his back. Ha! I love it!"

"I malign Plankton to his face, and he maligns me right back. You've heard his show. You know how these J-Bird people communicate with one another."

"Trading insults is how certain types of heterosexual men show affection for one another," Zinsser said. "Many gay men do too, in their own way. But you really mean it. You hate your employer. What a duplicitous asshole you are."

"Actually, Plankton's not too crazy about me either, and says so sincerely. In any case, I've taken the job mainly as a favor to an old acquaintance, a New York City cop who once saved my life. He thinks my contacts with the old FFF might help me sort out this current thing."

Zinsser laughed. "And so you've come over here thinking I might have Leo Moyle trussed up in a dungeon behind my root cellar. Is that it?"

"You were not selected as a suspect randomly, Zinsser. The neo-FFFers, as you may know, have been harassing Jay Plankton for several weeks with insults and rude items sent to him through the mail. One of the substances, labeled 'excrement for the execrable,' has been identified under scientific analysis as llama shit. Any idea where it might have come from? I'm sure your supply here is ample."

He hesitated just perceptibly as something seemed to go through his mind. Then he said quickly, "If that's somebody's idea of advancing the cause of gay rights, it sounds ineffective to me. I can certainly assure you I had nothing to do with anything so juvenile, and so perfectly lame. As I said, I've got to be in Great Barrington in twenty minutes. But you're welcome to scour the premises here in search of Leo Moyle bound and gagged, if that's what you've come all this way for. Feel free to turn the place inside out."

"Thanks. I would like to look around. Eliminate you as a suspect or whatever."

Zinsser checked his watch. "Darren can show you around. Darren's my partner. Although, he can't leave the visitors' center for long. People show up and want to see the operation and sample the product."

"Do visitors always take to your cheese immediately, or does eating it require some getting used to?"

"Nearly all our visitors," Zinsser said with a look of satisfaction, "are longtime customers before they arrive. For many of them, coming here is a kind of pilgrimage."

"And the Berkshires, luckily, are more convenient than the Andes."

"I should say hello to Thad," Zinsser said, quickly backing away now toward his pickup truck. "But I'm going to be late for a meeting if I don't get moving. Tell Thad I'm sorry I missed him. What's he doing now, anyway?"

"Farming. In central New Jersey."

"That sounds wholesome enough," Zinsser said, climbing into his truck. "He's not raising llamas, is he?"

"No, mostly eggplants."

"Ah, is moussaka an Amish dish?" Zinsser said. "Who would have guessed." He waved once and drove off fast.

CHAPTER 13

Timmy said, "We're onto something here."

"You bet we are," Thad added.

"We are?"

No sooner had Zinsser departed than Timmy and Thad emerged from the barn picking hair out of their teeth. As we spoke, they repeatedly spit into Zinsser's parking lot, which I now noticed was strewn with tiny strands of gnarled wool.

"Zinsser's boyfriend Darren, who's in there reading an ancient Incan text while he's minding the cash register," Timmy said, "gave us the lowdown on three kids who work for Zinsser during the week making cheese."

"They're trouble," Thad said, "and Zinsser is actually meeting a couple of other guys in Great Barrington right now that he wants to hire to replace these kids he doesn't get along with."

"These three," Timmy went on, "are young and gay and angry and out of control, according to Darren. And, not only do they have constant personality and ideological clashes with Zinsser, recently they fought over which radio station to have on in the cheese-making room during the morning. The kids want WRPI for the music they like and the Pacifica news. Zinsser is always present to supervise— apparently getting the wool-to-cheese blend just right can be tricky—and he insists that the radio be tuned into . . . guess who?"

"Interesting."

"And so," Thad said, "there's this constant tension in the morning, with the kids—their names are Charm, Pheromone and Edward—mocking and berating Jay Plankton all the time, and Zinsser refusing to change the station."

"Why haven't the kids quit? Or why hasn't Zinsser replaced them sooner?" I asked.

Timmy said, "They live up the road in Charm's father's house. He's one of Zinsser's financial backers. The father's in Provence for the summer with his new wife. But Charm can only live there and have her checking account replenished periodically if she's willing to work for Zinsser. She had academic and drug problems, and this is part of her rehab program. Zinsser has to keep her around—and where Charm goes, Pheromone and Edward go too—so he's canning the Mexican illegals who now do the field and barn chores, Darren says, and Zinsser's getting the three young people out into the open air where he won't have to listen to them dis the J-Bird all morning long."

I thought it over and said, "None of this is what I expected to find here." I described to Timmy and Thad my encounter with Kurt Zinsser, angry neolefty turned angry neocon. "Unless his devotion to Jay Plankton is all a cunning pose, which I don't think it is, Zinsser is as unlikely a harasser of Plankton or kidnapper of Leo Moyle as we're likely to come across. These kids do sound like better bets, sort of. Certainly they would have access to llama droppings. And if they couldn't stand Zinsser and wanted to mess with his mind and get away with it, they could go after his hero, the J-Bird. Except, of course, they're . . . kids. Three young students in rural Massachusetts who stage a kidnapping in New York? I don't know about that."

"But," Timmy said, "we haven't met them. Darren says they're pretty out of control. Especially Charm Stankewitz. And they know about Zinsser and the old FFF. He told them all about it, apparently hoping to show how cool he once was."

"Are Charm, Pheromone and Edward their real names?"

Thad casually spat something ugly into the dust and said, "Charm's real name is Patricia Stankewitz, and Edward's is Edward Nicetwink. It had been Edward Beers, but he had it legally changed last winter when he hit eighteen and his parents in Stockbridge couldn't stop him. Pheromone's actual name, believe it or not, is Pheromone Peabody."

"An old New England Yankee family via the sixties, it sounds like," Timmy said.

"And what about Darren, your source for all this data?" I asked. "I take it Darren strikes you as a reliable source of information."

"He's got no axe to grind that's evident," Timmy said. "He's Zinsser's boyfriend, and that's clearly where his sympathies lie. But his story of these three troubled youths is plausible enough."

"Why don't you go in and meet Darren?" Thad said. "He'll give you a free sample of Woolly Llama Cheese."

Timmy said, "Yes, you haven't had any yet."

"Is it pretty awful?"

"Of course," they said, nearly in unison.

"Lead the way."

Darren, a slender, sloe-eyed man a good twenty years Zinsser's junior, was wearing a llama T-shirt like his partner's. He had a small llama tattoo on one upper arm, and on the other upper arm were tattooed the words "Robert Forever," apparent evidence of the hazards of subdermal body decoration.

At my request, Darren reiterated what he had told Timmy and Thad about Charm, Pheromone and Edward. He had nothing new to add, although when I asked him directly whether he thought these three schoolkids—Pheromone was only seventeen, and Edward and Charm just a year older—were capable of pulling off a kidnapping, Darren said, "Nothing those brats did would surprise me. They are totally unpredictable, and I've always thought truly dangerous."

"But how could they kidnap anybody in New York? Are any of them big enough and tough enough to wrestle a man in his forties into a waiting vehicle? Do they possess firearms or other weapons, or drugs they could use on somebody?"

"I don't know about guns," Darren said, "but I suppose they could drug someone. All three of them have extensive experience with pharmaceuticals. They're all rather small, but if they were going to snatch somebody in New York they might have larger friends there who could help them. They go into the city at least once a week and stay with some people in Brooklyn."

"Any idea who these people are?"

"Not really. I've heard them mention Louis somebody, and a Sharon, I think, and somebody they refer to as Strawberry Swirl."

You could practically hear the wheels turn as we all made mental notes on Louis, Sharon and Strawberry Swirl.

"Were Charm, Pheromone and Edward in the city yesterday?" I asked. "That's when the kidnapping took place. Late morning sometime."

"Actually, I think they were," Darren said, his eyes widening. "Or Charm was anyway. We weren't making cheese yesterday. We won't make cheese again until Tuesday. By then Kurt thinks he'll have some new people to work for us who are less obnoxious to have around."

Timmy said, "Don, you haven't tried any cheese yet."

"No," Thad added. "We have but you haven't."

Darren got up from his stool behind the counter. "This stuff will change your life," he said, with no trace of irony. His was supposed to be the generation steeped in irony, but apparently that had all gone by him. Using a small square of parchment paper, Darren retrieved a sample-sized portion of Berkshire Woolly Llama Cheese from the refrigerator case. It was grayish, and it resembled a mouse minus its extremities.

"You're serving this cheese chilled," I said. "Shouldn't it be allowed to warm to the task of being eaten, to collect its cheesy thoughts for a while?"

"Ideally, yes," Darren said. "But much of the flavor and nearly all of the healing properties are in the oil of the wool. As you suck the cheese out of the wool, the chewing and sucking combined with the heat of your own saliva release the oil and its protein. One of the sad aspects of modern American life is the haste with which most people devour their food. It was easier for the ancient Incas, of course, to take the time to absorb the healing oils in their llama cheese, because they lived a much less pressured existence."

As I inserted the moist morsel into my mouth, Thad said, "Rural agricultural people have plenty of pressure on them, usually associated with the vagaries of climate. But it is true that the pace of that life is much slower a lot of the time."

"The trouble with the hectic lives we lead," Timmy said, "is that for most of us it's all too rare that we take the time to stop and suck the cheese."

Which was what I was doing at that moment. The

cheese itself wasn't bad—ripe, a little salty, with a hint of smoke, and not so gluey as I feared. The wool that was marbled through it, however, was another matter. I was counting on my finely tuned gag reflex to prevent disaster. What if I swallowed this thing whole? Had that ever happened to a Berkshire Woolly Llama Cheese devotee? Were there FDA warnings on the package?

I glanced around the shop for a Heimlich-maneuver instructions poster. None was visible, although I knew Timmy was capable of successfully executing the procedure. Some years earlier I had seen him apply the maneuver and dislodge what looked like half a strip steak from an old lady's trachea at a Friendly's restaurant near Lake George. So adept was Timmy that upon the first upward thrust under the desperate woman's rib cage, the deadly gob was ejected and shot across the room, knocking over a little boy's Fribble®.

"What do you think?" Thad said.

"It's tasty," I replied. "But sucking a wad of hair takes some getting used to. It's uncommon in our culture."

Timmy said, "Thad, do the Amish chew hair?"

"Not in Pennsylvania, as far as I ever heard. In Indiana maybe they do, or Ohio."

Darren said, "To achieve the full benefits, you really need to eat it every day for several weeks."

Almost as if by plan, we quickly changed the subject back to Charm, Pheromone and Edward, and discussed how we would carry out a visit to them at Charm's father's house up the road.

CHAPTER 14

"You can ask us anything you want to ask," Charm Stankewitz said, blowing clove-cigarette smoke in my direction.
"But anything we don't feel like talking about, we're not
going to talk about. Got that? It'll be up to us, not you, what
subjects are covered. If you want to talk about J-Bird Plankton, maybe we'll answer your questions, and maybe we
won't. Just so you understand what the rules are before we
get started with this . . . this whatever."

Charm, Pheromone, Edward and I were seated in the
living room/dining room of the converted carriage house
near the main Stankewitz house, a gorgeous federal-style
former farmhouse that looked as if it had been painted
white just minutes before. The building we were in, apparently a guest house being occupied for the summer by

Charm and her friends, was nicely furnished with an assortment of comfortable antique and reproduction nineteenth-century New England country furnishings. The building's current occupants had added some touches of their own, too. A large sound system and a rack full of CDs were perched on the mahogony sideboard, and an array of posters touting queer and feminist causes had been taped to the picture molding. One poster, vividly illustrated, advertised something called the "Penn State Cuntfest."

Timmy and Thad had remained outside, out of sight. Timmy was in the car, parked at the end of the lane leading to the Stankewitz house, scoping out who came and went. Thad was to use his FFF guerrilla skills to surreptitiously check out a barn and several smaller outbuildings on the property, whose name, according to a discreet sign hung from a post, was Beech Hill.

I had decided to use a direct approach with Charm, Pheromone and Edward. They were unloading groceries from a Jeep Cherokee when I strolled up to them, identified myself as a private investigator looking into Leo Moyle's kidnapping by the Forces of Free Faggotry, and told them that Kurt Zinsser's old FFF connections had led me to the Berkshire Woolly Llama Cheese farm and its employees. Pheromone and Edward had looked startled—near panic was evident just beneath the surface of Edward's frozen gaze—but Charm hardly blinked and immediately invited me into the carriage house. She welcomed me to Bitch Hill and handed me a case of Budweiser to carry up the steps.

"I think it's hilarious," Charm said, "that you think you might find out anything about Leo Moyle's kidnapping from Kurt, that neofascist chucklehead. Politically, he hasn't been able to get it up for about a thousand years, and anyway Jay Plankton and his gang of right-wing enforcers are cultural icons of Kurt's. I'm having a lot of trouble conceptualizing a role for Kurt in what sounds to me like an authentic act of people's justice."

Charm blew more clove-flavored smoke, and Edward and Pheromone sat and stared at me. Charm was slight and wiry in yellow shorts and an orange tank top, with a pug nose, breasts to match, intelligent green eyes and a buzz cut. Pheromone and Edward had the same basic haircut as Charm's, but both were taller, wore jeans and T-shirts, and had long faces with an assortment of studs and rings affixed to them. I could have hung Grandma Strachey's entire set of Christmas tree ornaments on Edward without having to puncture his skin additionally. All three of them were tattooed like sailors out of Jean Genet, with some of the graphics, such as barbed armbands, of the in-your-face variety, and others, among them small anthropods and amphibians, benign or even friendly.

I said to Charm, "I see your point about Kurt. He seems to have turned into Andrew Sullivan with wool in his teeth. But it wasn't just Kurt's history with the FFF that led me here."

I described the harassment-by-mail series of incidents that led up to Leo Moyle's abduction, including the arrival on Jay Plankton's desk of a carton of llama turds, "excrement for the execrable." As I spoke, Charm eyed me coolly, while Pheromone fidgeted and Edward perspired and grew whiter and whiter.

"That's a riot," Charm said after I'd run through the alphabetical list ending in "*H* for hostage." She puffed on her exotic cigarette and added, "I hope that the *I* attack is 'irritants for the irritating' or even 'injuries for the injurious.'"

Pheromone and Edward both flinched at this, and I said, "Deliberately injuring someone is a felony. You can go to jail for battery."

"We really wouldn't *hurt* anybody," Pheromone blurted out, and her brown eyes misted up.

"And kidnapping," I went on, "is a federal crime sometimes punishable by death. Personally, I'm against capital punishment for both practical and moral reasons, but the US government is still in no mood to join me and the rest of the civilized world in this regard. Whatever his private inclinations, Clinton goes along with public opinion, which remains predominantly bloodthirsty, and Al Gore shows no sign of deviating from the harsh party line. And, of course, should George W. Bush be elected president—which has to be considered both laughable and highly unlikely—you can be assured that he will do at the national level what he has done in Texas. Which has been to snicker as he casually balls up clemency petitions and lobs them into the nearest wastebasket. Kidnappers, now and for the forseeable future in the United States, can frequently expect to be dispatched to kingdom come via lethal injection, electrocution or firing squad with a minimum of ceremony. Kidnappers who haven't thought about these consequences are making a disastrous mistake."

Pheromone wore a look of horror, and poor Edward, whose only word to me so far had been a barely audible "hi," seemed about to burst into tears. I was not enjoying making these two young people suffer, but my approach did seem as though it would serve to expedite the investigation I had agreed to conduct.

Charm was unimpressed by my theatrics, however, and said so. "You talk such a load of shit, Strachey. If you're trying to get us to confess to assaulting anybody or kidnapping Leo Moyle, you're wasting your time and ours. As much as I savor the picture of that misogyno-fascist Moyle strung up by his tiny balls in some cellar full of rats, I can promise you we *wouldn't* do it ourselves, and we *didn't* do it ourselves, or with anyone else. What do you take us for? Do we look like the Tupac Amaru, or what?"

This denial was couched with such exquisitely evasive calculation—Charm Stankewitz was going to make a great

White House chief of staff someday—that what should have been obvious for some time now hit me like a ton of Woolly Llama Cheese.

I said, "So the three of you carried out the harassment of Jay Plankton, but not the kidnapping of Leo Moyle? Is that what you're telling me?"

"We're not telling you *anything*," Charm said emphatically, "but if you want to draw the harmless conclusion of your choice and then be on your way, that would be so-o-o-o cool. Am I making myself sufficiently clear?"

Pheromone and Edward watched me with a look of hope. I said to them, "Your friend Charm is a brilliantly precocious advocate for your various good causes. I just hope she doesn't lead you into . . . well, I'm sure you've given it a lot of thought. Some remote cell block in the Peruvian penal system, or—more likely—the newly redecorated federal execution suite in Terre Haute."

"Shit!" This was Edward.

"Oh God!" That was Pheromone.

"Charm's right, we *didn't* kidnap that guy," Edward said plaintively.

"Fuck, no," Pheromone added, underlining the declaration.

"But you sent menacing and repellent notes and substances to Jay Plankton through the mail?"

Charm sat examining her dark cigarette and looking blasé, while Pheromone and Edward gave their final freeze-frame look of fear.

"And you filled Plankton's SUV full of toilet paper during a party at his manager's house in Mamaroneck?"

Before Pheromone and Edward had the chance to faint, or shriek and bolt out the door, Charm said, "Sure we did, and *so what!*"

"I'm no fan of Plankton's either, but you may have broken a few laws."

Charm sneered. "Plankton and his stupid little boys are

floaters in the malfunctioning toilet of American broadcasting. What we did was good for the J-Bird and Leo Moyle, and I think it is totally terrific that somebody obviously took our cue and went after these rotten turds in the manner they deserve. Down in the cheese room, we had to listen to these assholes day after day after day, while Kurt ha-haed and hee-heed. I mean, what were we supposed to do, call OSHA? Yes, we did it, and we're *proud* we did it!"

This last statement may have been too sweeping for Pheromone and Edward, who still stared at me apprehensively. I said, "And you lobbed the tear-gas canister into Plankton's studio yesterday?"

"No way!" Pheromone exclaimed. "We, like, mailed in that shit and stuff, but we didn't throw tear gas, and we never kidnapped that guy, no way!"

Edward also became more vocal. "We just wanted to fuck with Kurt's mind. He's a Republican now, but he talks about his FFF days like he's some Greatest Generation hero, wiping up the floor with Nazis. I mean, like, the movie about the FFF will have Tom Hanks in it playing Kurt. This guy is totally fucked up, and we were just giving him a hard time about it, that's all."

"Then you might or might not be happy to know," I told them, "that until Leo Moyle was kidnapped, Jay Plankton thought of you all as brothers and sisters under the skin, and admirably insolent and hugely entertaining. He talked about putting you all on his show—pending the outcome, of course, of a pre-interview and probably an exhaustive strip search."

"Well, that sucks!" Pheromone said.

"What a bunch of perverts," Edward added.

But Charm had grown thoughtful. "And now he's changed his mind?" she asked. "Because of the Leo Moyle thing?"

"That would be my guess."

"Oh."

"You can ask him yourself, if you're interested. I'm sure he'll be wanting to be in touch with you. His attorneys will, anyway, along with the police and the FBI. If you didn't do the kidnapping, or even the tear-gas job, it'll probably be easy enough for you to prove it. And if eventually you do go on the air with the J-Bird, I know I'll be sure to tune in."

Pheromone said, "Going on the radio is for shit, so don't try to drag me in on this one, Charm. But I suppose we'll have to tell them we didn't do it. The tear gas or the kidnapping, I mean. We can give them some of our DNA—though I'll bet it's hard to prove a negative unless the J-Bird was, like, raped."

Charm was looking even more worried. "Do you think we'll need a lawyer?"

"That might be wise," I said.

"Shit. I'll have to call Dad in Nîmes. He's going to be spitting afterbirth."

On that vivid note, I advised Charm, Pheromone, and Edward to stay put in the Berkshires. I told them that flight from official investigators would be inadvisable. I suggested they tell Kurt Zinsser what they had done and to say that he should expect the police to show up shortly. The three of them took all of this in sullenly, but they all seemed to get my drift and they didn't argue.

Back outside, Thad was just returning to the car. He told me he had given the main house, the barn and the other Stankewitz outbuildings an apparently undetected quick scouring, inside and out, and he could find no trace of Leo Moyle or any other person. He said all the Stankewitz locks were old and simple and "a piece of cake."

Inside the car, though, Timmy was itching to give us his own amazing report. He had been monitoring WCBS all-news radio from New York, and moments earlier he had heard that Leo Moyle had just been released by the FFF largely unharmed. But now Jay Plankton himself had been abducted.

CHAPTER 15

"It was a beautiful operation," Lyle Barner was telling me. "It could have been carried out by the finest SWAT team in the country, or maybe by the Mossad. Here, this guy's got some of the best security in the city, outside of the Secret Service when Clinton's in town, and these people move in and snatch Plankton up like he's a calzone at Sbarro, and just like that—kapooey!—the J-Bird is up in smoke."

This was said in a Chinese restaurant on Sixty-fifth Street, not far from Jay Plankton's apartment building, at the entrance to which he had been abducted seven hours earlier. Thad and I had dropped Timmy off back in Albany and driven to the city in Thad's truck. Thad and I agreed that for the time being he should steer clear of Barner, so he said he would go spend the night with an old Lancaster

County friend in Brooklyn. I had asked him if there was an Amish ethnic enclave in one of the outer boroughs, like the Polish in Greenpoint or the Indians in Jackson Heights, but he said no.

"It was like they'd rehearsed it a hundred times," Barner went on. "At least fourteen people saw the whole thing, and they all said it happened so fast that nobody really knew what had gone down, until Moyle started yelling that he was Leo Moyle of the *Jay Plankton Show*, and he'd been kidnapped and let go and somebody should summon an officer."

The switch—Moyle for Plankton—had indeed been deft, Barner told me. As the security-service Bronco carrying Plankton pulled up at the entrance to the apartment building and Plankton stepped out with his two armed guards, a second SUV, a green Lincoln Navigator, came up from behind. Two men in black jeans, black turtlenecks and gas masks emerged and fired pepper spray at Plankton and his protectors and at the Bronco's driver. It sounded to me like the feds swooping in and snatching little Elián González in Miami, overpowering Donato-the-fisherman-slash-cleaning-service-operator, and gassing the praying grandmothers in front of the house. I wondered, Did I detect the fine hand of Janet Reno here? Much as the Clinton administration must have loathed the J-Bird, an abduction by Justice Department paramilitaries didn't sound like the answer.

An NYPD patrol car arrived at the scene within two minutes of Moyle's release and the J-Bird's capture, Barner said, but the Navigator had made a clean getaway. By the time a description of the vehicle went out, the kidnappers had apparently switched cars. For the Lincoln was soon spotted abandoned under the FDR Drive near Thirty-eighth Street. The car had been stolen earlier that morning, police soon discovered, from in front of a real estate office in New Rochelle. One potential witness thought she had seen the switch from the Navigator to a gray, brown or light blue van, but the description was too vague to be of any help.

Moyle, Barner told me, was taken by patrol car to Lenox Hill Hospital, where he was examined and found to be exhausted but not physically harmed in any serious way. His mental state, however, was described as precarious. This was owing in part to the fearful ordeal overall, but in particular to his two newly acquired tattoos, one on each upper arm. They were both large, still fresh, and a little sore. One pictured big red lips and said, "Kiss Me, Elton". The other said, "I ♥ Ricky Martin".

The tattoos had been applied to Moyle involuntarily while he was tied down, blindfolded, and had a gun held to his head, he told police. He pleaded that word of his new body art not be made public. But Barner, who arrived on the scene twenty minutes after the first patrol car, had to break it to Moyle that the news would almost certainly leak out, probably via hospital employees. Anyway, the issue was soon moot, for the kidnappers—or their friends or coconspirators—dropped off digital photos of Moyle's new look at the lobbies of the *Times*, the *Post* and the *Daily News*. This suggested to Barner, and to me, that more than a few people were involved in whatever was going on here. No ransom note had yet been received by anyone the police knew of. So far, the tattoos were the only message.

Barner said he didn't know much about tattoos, and he asked me, "Can tattoos be removed, or are people stuck with them for the rest of their lives?"

"I don't know," I told him, "but in Massachusetts I ran into a guy who had a tattoo on his arm that said 'Robert Forever', and Robert had turned out to be less than forever. But the tattoo was still there, so maybe they're hard to shed."

Barner and I were set to meet with Moyle in an hour or so, after his release from Lenox Hill, and tattoo removal seemed to both of us a subject Moyle would be eager to discuss.

I said to Barner, "The tabloids are going to have a lot of fun with this. They undoubtedly adore Moyle at the *Post,* but public humiliation of a C-list celeb is their meat, and the festering tattoo work sounds to me like surefire page-one stuff. I'm sure that at this very moment the *Post* has a reporter assigned to getting a quote from Ricky Martin."

Barner looked up from his egg-drop soup. "Moyle's an asshole, yeah, I know. But I really feel kind of sorry for him."

"Why?"

"You know—just what he went through."

"I agree that terrorizing the guy is going way too far," I said. "Moyle must have feared for his life. But as for the tattoos . . . that's a nice, droll touch. The raging homophobe forced to go around with the brand of Oscar Wilde."

Barner peered at me glumly. "Jesus, Strachey, you're merciless. How would you like it if somebody snatched you and tattooed you with 'Strachey's Hot for Pamela Anderson'?"

"I haven't made a career of denigrating straight women, so the chances of that happening are slight. If it did happen, it wouldn't be rough justice. It would just be absurdist."

"You can call it whatever weird crap you want to," Barner said, "but getting forcibly tattooed like that would make anybody feel like shit. That's all I'm saying. Moyle is an asshole, but he's also a human being."

"Lyle, if Moyle knew you were gay, and it was you who got embroidered—let's say, 'Lyle Is Hot for Al D'Amato'—how sympathetic do you think Moyle would be? Can't you imagine him and Plankton and the fun they'd have on the air with news of a gay NYPD detective involuntarily tattooed?"

"Yeah, that's so. But still . . . anyway, what would your boyfriend say about it? Didn't you tell me one time he was some kind of priest who forgot to go to seminary or something? He sounds like a much nicer person than you are, Strachey."

"He is," I said, without having to think about that one. "And I'm sure Timothy will share your opinion on this subject, Lyle."

"And what about Thad-the-Amishman that you're cheating on your boyfriend with? He brags about how he never hurt anybody when he was in the FFF. What do you think Thad's going to say about somebody committing battery on Leo Moyle? Is Thad, the man of peace, gonna just laugh it off, like you?"

I decided to ignore most of this—probably confirming my guilt and duplicity in Barner's mind—and said only, "Yes, Thad's opinion of the tattooing will be closer to yours and Timmy's than to mine. That's true, Lyle. We'll just have to agree to disagree."

This last sounded like some namby-pamby remark from a hack pol on "Sam and Cokie," and Barner had me on the edge of feeling guilty all over again over the way I treated him. But then Barner said this: "I know Diefendorfer was with you in Albany and Massachusetts. So, what have you got going, a threesome? Normally I'm too square for that type of kinky stuff. Just ask Dave. But with you and Thad, maybe I could start to act more with it. Timothy Callahan is a very, very lucky man, in my opinion."

I peered at Barner for a long moment. "You had someone—what? Watching me? Following me?"

Barner colored just perceptibly but looked at me levelly. "I guess you got to know Diefendorfer quite intimately, Strachey. But maybe you didn't get to know him intimately enough."

"Wait a minute, Lyle. We'll come back to that. Just answer my question. Did you or did you not put a tail on me when I traveled to Albany and Massachusetts yesterday and today?"

The waiter arrived and removed our soup dishes. Then he was back within seconds, and he set down a large dish of rice along with Barner's General Tso's chicken—who was this warrior with a taste for sweet, sticky fowl, anyway?— and my shrimp with mushrooms and snow peas.

When the waiter was gone, Barner said, "Why don't you tell me first, Strachey, did you or didn't you forget to let me in on the fact that your partner working on this case was going to be not myself but somebody else, not even a professional investigator, and that person would be the humpy Dutchman, Thad Diefendorfer? As I understood it, we would be working together, one of the reasons I brought you onto the case. And now—I guess you can tell, because I'm making myself pretty fucking crystal clear—I am all stressed out about this, and I am feeling royally fucked over."

So there I was. I had chosen not to let Barner in on Diefendorfer's involvement in the investigation because I knew that if he knew about it, Lyle would act like a child— i.e., jealous, resentful, distracted, suspicious and petulant. How had I let myself become entangled in this miasma? Oh, right. Barner had once saved my life. Why couldn't it have been somebody else that violent summer night in Albany fifteen years earlier who had bailed me out of a desperate fix—Rex the Wonder Horse, or Miss Marple?

I said to Barner, "Thad was tagging along with me, yes, to be helpful if he could. But you were . . . you were *spying* on me. I have to say, Lyle, that I am at this moment disgusted with you."

My strained tactic of displaying moral outrage that might trump Barner's moral outrage did not impress him. For which I was grateful, because I was growing bored with each of us acting morally superior to the other for no very good reason.

Barner said simply, "I had two officers tail you, yeah. It was partly to keep me informed, and it was also to drag your ass out of the smoke and flames if that was to become necessary. Like I did on the Millpond case back in Albany.

These two young officers did a nice job, too. You never had a clue." He grinned and dug into his gooey chicken.

I said, "Are they still up there, these two young officers? Are they the ones checking out Charm and her gang, and Kurt Zinsser—who, by the way, no law-enforcement agency would ever have known about had it not been for me?"

"No, my officers tailed you and the Amish eggplant stud back to the city. I sent another detective up to work with the state police detectives out of Springfield to talk to the cheese-farm vandals. I should have a report from them later tonight."

I said, "You mentioned that it was your opinion, Lyle, that I had not come to know Thad Diefendorfer intimately enough. First, let's get it straight that I have not been physically intimate with Thad. Neither has Timmy, heaven forfend. It's a nice scene to contemplate, but the stars of Timmy's and my zodiac are not so aligned at present. So why don't you just get all the sex stuff involving me, and Thad, and you out of your head? Let's all proceed not in the realm of fantasy but with our feet on the ground in the real world."

Barner sniffed. He was sure I was lying through my teeth. It was sad.

I went on. "But you seemed to be suggesting, Lyle, that intimate knowledge of Thad's behavior—as opposed to, say, intimate knowledge of his nice butt—would be important for me to obtain. What did you mean by that?"

Barner paused for dramatic effect—Fritz Lang must once have taught a course at the police academy—and said, "After Diefendorfer dropped you off at the J-Bird's place, my team followed him over to Brooklyn. He parked his pickup truck on Lorimer Street in Williamsburg and entered a nearby apartment building. The super was in the lobby when Diefendorfer went in, and my officers were able to determine that the subject—that would be your buddy Thaddie—was admitted to a second-floor apartment whose tenant's name meant something to me when I heard it.

"While you were up in Massachusetts, Strachey, I went over the FBI file on the old FFF. One of Mr. Diefendorfer's cohorts in 1975–76 was a man by the name of Sam Day. The lessee of the Lorimer Street apartment is Sam Day. Sam Day, the super told my officers, is the leader of some type of organization, with people coming and going from that apartment at all hours of the day and night, especially night. I don't think Jay Plankton is being held there. The super says the apartment is small, only one bedroom. But as a precaution I've got the place under twenty-four-hour surveillance. So what do you think of them apples, Detective Strachey?"

Damned if I knew. Barner was now sounding almost borderline-deranged. But it was funny that Thad had not mentioned to me that the "Lancaster County" friend he was visiting in Brooklyn was his onetime boyfriend in the FFF.

CHAPTER 16

Moyle lived in a sixties-era white-brick high-rise on Seventy-fourth near Third, and that's where Barner and I met him. He had been spirited out of Lenox Hill Hospital in an ambulance past a mob of reporters and television news vans, then transferred to an NYPD patrol car three blocks away. With the private security force guarding Jay Plankton having screwed up grandly, Moyle was now under the protection of the police.

Jerry Jeris had joined us in Moyle's living room for his second debriefing of the day, the feds having had a go at Moyle at Lenox Hill. Jurisdiction was unclear at this point—had either abductee actually been transported across a state line?—but while Moyle was a relatively minor player in the nation's cultural life, J-Bird Plankton was a man who had twice appeared on the cover of *People*. As such, any crime against his person was almost by definition a federal offense, if only honorary, and automatically triggered the involvement of the FBI, if not the Department of Defense.

"For fuck's sake," Moyle was saying as soon as he lit up a cigar, "this is my first smoke in thirty-six hours. These terrorists, not only did they deprive me of a single decent meal—the meatball sub they fed me last night was for shit—the bastards wouldn't even buy me a cheap smoke, and here I'm afraid for my very life and I'm going into friggin' nicotine withdrawal on top if it."

"What sadists," Jeris said, and lit up too.

The black-glass coffee table had three ashtrays lined up on it, each the size of a meteorite crater but not as clean. The beige leather couch and chairs to match faced a television set that could have been used for the return of Cinerama, though thankfully it was turned off. Moyle was sucking up his rehabilitative smoke, but apparently he was not going to insist that our questioning of him be conducted while ESPN played reassuringly in the background. On other cases, I had seen that happen.

"Anyway," Moyle said to Jeris, "a fat lot of help you and Glodt were while I'm locked in some toxic dump in Jersey or someplace with no smokes, and sawdust for meatballs, and these deranged fags mutilating me and threatening to eat my pancreas for lunch if I don't do what they tell me. I heard what the reward was from Steve—a niggerly six-five—and J. Pukingham Christ, I couldn't fucking believe my ears. Except, of course, knowing Steve, I sure as shit could believe it, and did. Steve the big spender. Steve the bleeding heart. Steve the Brooke Astor of New York AM radio."

"At first it was five," Jeris said. "But Jay and I pleaded with Steve, we were practically kissing his skinny butt, and he said okay, then six-five. For Steve, that's not small. He says he's gonna have to raise the national ad rates in October to get his money back if anybody claims the reward."

I said, "Leo, why did you think you might have been taken to New Jersey? You told the officers who picked you up outside Jay Plankton's apartment this afternoon that you had been blindfolded while you were in transit. But now you say you might have been held in New Jersey. Why is that?"

Moyle was only vaguely aware of who I was. He knew that I was a private investigator who had once had contacts with the FFF, that I had been hired by Jeris and Plankton, and that I was working with NYPD. He peered over at me with his small gray eyes and said, "We were either in Jersey or Queens because we went through a tunnel going, and we came through a tunnel coming back. It sounded like traffic in a tunnel, and my ears popped."

Jeris said, "Hey, Leo, they popped your ears, but at least they didn't pop your cherry." Jeris chuckled, while Moyle considered this somberly and didn't chuckle back. He wasn't ready to get back into the old J-Bird routine just yet.

Barner said, "Yeah, Jersey or Queens, maybe. Lincoln, Holland, Queens Midtown. What about Brooklyn Battery? Could it've been Brooklyn?"

"Could've been Brooklyn, yeah," Moyle said. "I couldn't tell. I'm so freakin' scared, I'm not exactly playing 'Name that Tunnel.' But going out, we go through the tunnel, then we drive for maybe an hour, maybe two, I don't know. It's on expressways, though, with some slowing down and speeding up, and no stop-and-go till we're almost where we're going. The same coming back, except in reverse.

"What kind of vehicle, I don't know, as I told the feds. At first it's some Bronco, or like that, that I was shoved into. But then after a couple of minutes they switched—this is before the tunnel, still in the city—and I don't know what I'm in. I'm on the floor of some van or delivery truck, blindfolded, tape over my mouth, and trussed up tighter than Steve Glodt's account at Brooklyn Dime."

"Which isn't probaby going to get any looser," Jeris said. "Not for the six-five reward anyhoo. I mean, who's going to claim it? The FFF assholes who snatched you and then let you go? That would take balls."

"Well, balls these pricks definitely have," Moyle said. "Light in the loafers they may be, but I can't say these friggin' sissy-boys don't have guts."

I said, "Were the kidnappers wearing loafers?"

"What?"

"Never mind. You were blindfolded."

"I was the entire time. I never saw their shoes. They untied my hands when we got to their place, but I never saw daylight for twenty-four hours. I felt like I was in a tomb and it could have been my own."

Barner said, "How did you know how much was being offered as a reward?"

"They had the radio on—WINS," Moyle said. "I was in this one hot room the whole time, no air conditioner even, just a fan and a radio. I was on a couch that smelled like somebody spilled some chick's nail polish on it. I just had to sit there or lay down to sleep, with my feet tied to the leg of the couch. I hardly got any sleep at all. I didn't know what these perverted creeps were gonna do to me next, ampute my hemorrhoids or extract my bottom teeth. There were two of them who did all the talking, and this one guy really liked to bust my nuts, tell me I was a homophobic shithead, and I was gonna pay for my sins."

"Those were the words the kidnapper used?" I asked. " 'Homophobic shithead' and 'pay for your sins'?"

"Yeah. The fag scumbag."

Jeris cleared his throat theatrically, but it went right by Moyle. He was back on his own turf and figured he could unwind and work on getting back to being himself.

I said, "The two who spoke—was there anything distinctive about their voices?"

"You mean like, did they lithp? No."

"They were both adult men?"

"Yeah."

"New Yorkers?"

"How do you mean?"

"Did either man have an accent? Brooklyn? Queens? Locust Valley lockjaw?"

"No," Moyle said. "They just talked regular American English, like me."

Moyle in fact had a mild South Boston accent, as if his vocal cords had been replaced early in life by a kazoo that somebody had stepped on. I said, "Did they sound like they were from Boston?"

"Oh. I dunno. I guess not, no."

"Were there any other voices that you heard, male or female?"

"No women," Moyle said. "But everybody was mostly, like, in another room. I might have heard a woman out there at one time. But I couldn't make out what anybody was talking about. There was always one of them in my room holding a gun on me, they said. They untied my hands, but I didn't try anything because twice this one sadist pushed a gun barrel against my forehead and said to cooperate or he'd blow my brains right through the wall. This was the one that really scared the piss out of me. He called me a sinner and an unrighteous man. This one wouldn't even let me take my blindfold off when I took a crap—God, I was practically having diarrhea—and he made me leave the bathroom door open while the pervert stands there and watches me take a shit."

I said, "He called you an 'unrighteous man'? Those were the words one of them used?"

Barner glanced my way, then back at Moyle, who said,

"Yeah, this one might have been a religious nut. A queer religious nut."

"What did these two call each other?" Barner said. "What names did they use?"

"No names," Moyle said, blowing cigar smoke. "I think they were being careful not to."

Barner said, "Did they mention Jay Plankton?"

"Oh, yeah. They had plenty to say about Jay and the show."

I said, "All unfavorable?"

"This one guy, the one who was busting my onions, he said when they got hold of Jay, Jay was gonna feel the pain. That's what the guy said, 'feel the pain.' He said my tattoos were nothing compared to what was in store for Jay. He said when I was released I should tell you all that."

"Who all?" I said. "You should tell who all that?"

"You all."

"Did he actually use our names?"

Moyle's beedy eyes all but disappeared as he considered this. "No," he said. "It was just, tell the cops. He didn't mention any names in particular."

Barner said, "Is it your impression that these people were planning on injuring the J-Bird? Is that what they were saying?"

"They could," Moyle said. "It sounded bad. They talked about sending Jay to a 'reeducation farm.' First they were going to take me to a reeducation farm, they said. But then they decided I wasn't reeducatable. I think that's when they decided to tattoo me and let me go, and to snatch Jay instead."

Jeris pointed his cigar at Moyle and said, "Leo, that's a great tribute to your manhood, if not your intelligence." Jeris grinned, but Moyle still wasn't quite ready for amusement at his own expense, and he just looked confused.

"Did they talk about the Forces of Free Faggotry?" I asked. "The FFF?"

"Oh yeah. Blah-*blah*, blah-*blah*, blah-*blah*. FFF this, FFF that. Last night, I'd had it up to here, and I told them, 'To me, you're all just a bunch of fucking fruit-cakes.' And I think that's when they decided I was hope-less, and unreeducatable."

"But," I said, "if you were unreeducatable, what made them think Plankton would be any different? You guys on the J-Bird show are famous for all being on the same wave-length. Especially on the subject of gays and gay rights."

Jeris was quick to cut in and say, "Don here is gay him-self, Leo. So be careful how you answer, ha-ha."

Moyle looked at me and said, "You don't look like a fag, Don. What're you doing, undercover work?"

I said, "And you do look like a fag, Leo. You've got love notes to Elton John and Ricky Martin tattooed on your upper arms. Things get confusing sometimes, don't they?"

Moyle reddened, and it was hard to tell which was stronger, his humiliation or his rage. As soon as he had entered his apartment, he had hiked up the air-conditioning and put on a New York Jets sweatshirt, covering up the infu-riating inkwork.

"I asked about it at Lenox Hill," Moyle said, crushing out his cigar butt. "Tattoos can be removed. It takes time, but I've already talked to one of the top dermatologists in New York—who's a huge fan of the show, by the way—and he says he can pretty much erase them. If I have to, I can have my own tattoos done on top of the residue of the ones these barbarians put on me. Pol Pot had nothing on these shitheads. They're going to pay too. Kidnapping and assault. I want their heads. I want their sick, perverted fag heads!" Moyle had begun to tremble, and a vein on his left temple was throbbing dangerously.

I said, "I guess you'll just have to get used to the fact, however, that your tattoos are going to live on in the annals of tabloid journalism. To help restore your mental health,

Leo, you might want to skip picking up tomorrow's *Post* and *Daily News*."

Moyle winced and looked even more agitated, but Jeris tried to help out. "Look at it this way, Leo: this is great juice for the show, once Jay gets back. Assuming he does come back, which I tend to think he will. That's because these FFFers, they're only talking about reeducating Jay, maybe roughing him up a little, like you say, but I'll bet not letting rats loose on his liver or any heavy shit like that. Look, Larry King's people called, and Fox, the *Today Show*—they all want you. Not Jay, but *you*, Leo. And Steve called and told me—he said, tell Leo to do 'em all; don't let even one opportunity slip away. Assuming you feel up to it, of course, which by Monday Steve is reasonably certain you will, and I am too.

"I mean, get some sleep, some brew, some pussy, and you'll be all set for some exposure. In fact, Steve wants you to do the show on Monday if Jay's not back. I've got the entire staff working on bookings. We'll get people who understand what you've been through, and can empathize, and who're still mad as hell over what happened to them. I'll get Patty Hearst, Lindbergh's daughter—what's her name—and some of the hostages from Iran and Lebanon like Terry Anderson. Or Loni. Was she kidnapped, too? Steve thinks this whole FFF thing is gonna do the show no harm at all—assuming, of course that you come out of it with your mental gazoomies intact, which appears to be the case, and that Jay does, too. Getting Jay back on the show Tuesday or Wednesday would be ideal, in fact.

"Detective Barner," Jeris said to Lyle, who had listened to this recitation with a look of wonder, "do you think it's possible, based on what you know of the FFF and Leo's experience, that your department can track down the kidnappers and get Jay sprung by, say, midweek?"

"Sooner than that is my intention," Lyle said. "It's my firm hope."

"Well, we could make anything work if we had to. Of course, Jay's well-being is uppermost."

Barner appeared to reflect on this. Moyle was gazing at Jeris thoughtfully, too, and looking not just shaken but also a little queasy.

CHAPTER 17

"Christ, it's another planet, these media guys," Barner was saying. "It's all ratings, and like that. This guy's been abducted, and what are his asshole buddies talking about? Juicing up the show, and who goes on the air, and how to cash in."

"Don't be too sweeping in your condemnation of the broadcast media, Lyle. I listen to National Public Radio, where I'm sure it's different. If Noah Adams was kidnapped, Linda Wertheimer and Robert Siegel wouldn't cynically sensationalize the event and turn into mike hogs. They'd offer themselves as substitute hostages, or at the very least recruit a group of public-spirited NPR underwriters to take Adams's place. Maybe Jennifer and Ted Stanley."

Barner, at the wheel of his NYPD unmarked Ford, let

this pass without comment. We were headed down the FDR toward the Williamsburg Bridge, and traffic was heavy and slow. I'd heard New Yorkers in Columbia County and the Berkshires talk about how the city empties out on summer weekends. Then, who was clogging the streets and highways on this steamy Saturday night in July? Had the population of Philadelphia been recruited to drive up and keep the New York bridge-and-tunnel toll collectors from growing bored and the asphalt from buckling owing to lack of use? It was a conundrum.

There was a more pressing puzzle, too. That was the question of Thad Diefendorfer's having neglected to inform me that the Lancaster County presumably Amish friend he was going to hang out with in Brooklyn was his old FFF boyfriend, Sammy Day. "Day" didn't sound Amish, but I supposed it could once have been Dazenburger or Dazenfeffer. Did Amish people who left their traditional communities behind for twenty-first–century life sometimes change their names as part of their assimilation? I didn't know.

And what was the business of one of Leo Moyle's captors accusing Moyle of being a sinner and an "unrighteous man"? What was that about? It didn't sound like FFF lingo, original or neo. It sounded downright Amish, in fact, according to what Diefendorfer had been telling me. And who were these people with their mysterious comings and goings at Sam Day's Brooklyn apartment at all hours of the day and night?

Maybe I would soon find out, because it's where Barner and I were en route to. We planned on simply knocking on the door and asking Diefendorfer and Day a series of pertinent questions. And, as a precaution, Barner had arranged to have additional police officers on hand should they be needed. Meanwhile, Barner also had a team of detectives checking out metropolitan-area tattoo artists, one of whom was apparently sufficiently angry at homophobes and radi-

calized enough to show up and do the inkwork on a kidnapped, bound, and blindfolded Leo Moyle on a Friday
night.

Barner tuned the car radio to WINS, where a variety of
New Yorkers, from Grand Central to Yankee Stadium,
offered comments to reporters on what WINS called the
"shocking" abduction of Jay Plankton. Some interviewees
weren't sure who Plankton was. One seemed to confuse
him with Howard Stern and another, inexplicably, with Al
Sharpton. But most knew of the J-Bird and seemed to
regard the kidnapping with a mixture of sympathy, concern
and bemusement. It wasn't, after all, as if Walter Cronkite
had been dragged off. There was one mild anti-FFF, antigay epithet that was allowed on the air and, in the interests
of what radio and television news professionals think of as
"balanced coverage," a gay man on Christopher Street pre-
senting a reap-what-you-sow argument.

Mayor Giuliani had appeared on the steps of city hall to
plead with the kidnappers to treat the J-Bird with "compas-
sion" and to remind them that if they harmed Plankton
they would have to pay a "very, very heavy price." One
resourceful reporter tracked down Ed Koch and asked his
opinion of the FFF. The sort of gay, semi-out former mayor
said the FFF meant well but had gone too far—"Violence is
never the answer"—and in any event was wasting its time
going after "a basically harmless gasbag like Jay Plankton."

Senatorial candidates Rick Lazio and Hillary Clinton
released nearly identical statements announcing that they
and their staffs and supporters were all praying for the
J-Bird's safety and early release. These prayers apparently
were private, for no vigils or services were planned by either
of the competing office-seekers.

Word of Leo Moyle's tattoos had already leaked, WINS
reported. A spokesman for Ricky Martin said the singer
would have no comment, but Elton John was quoted as saying he looked forward to a joint appearance with Moyle at

the next Academy Awards show. No one was sure if he was kidding. Moyle himself was described by WINS as "in seclusion" at his East Side apartment. Jerry Jeris told the station Moyle was grateful for the support and prayers of all the J-Bird show's fans, who, he said, should tune in on Monday to hear Moyle's description of his "night of terror" and his thoughts about it.

As we pulled onto the ramp for the old Erector-set contraption called the Williamsburg Bridge, Barner said, "Are you still pissed off at me?"

"Why?"

"For fucking up the thing you had going with your farmboy crush, that hottie Thaddie."

"I'm not happy, Lyle, that you were operating behind my back. But I was operating behind yours to a certain extent, so what can I say?" Barner glanced my way as we hurtled across the vibrating old steel span. "That's a rare admission for you, Strachey. What's come over you?"

"But apparently I need to explain to you one more time, Lyle—or twenty-five more times, if that's what it takes—that I am not now having, nor have I ever had, nor do I ever intend to have, a romantic relationship with Thad Diefendorfer. I concede that my erotic life may once have resembled that of Patti Smith and her band. But with the rare, odd, innocuous deviation, the life Timothy Callahan and I now lead most resembles that of Gerald and Betty Ford. So if you don't mind, you can just knock off the hot Thaddie routine."

With no particular inflection, Barner said, "You're lying."

I could think of no reply as we rumbled down onto the ancient streets of Brooklyn. After a moment, I asked Lyle, "What's with you and Dave tonight? Speaking of nonexistent threesomes, or fivesomes, or whatever it isn't."

"Nothing's with Dave and me tonight," Barner said. "I'm on duty, obviously, and he's out on the Island somewhere with . . . with his poppers and his God-knows-what-other-mind-altering-substances and some other guys. I wasn't invited this time."

"About which you are probably ambivalent."

"Yeah."

"When will you see him again?"

"It depends," Barner said. "I heard from my captain earlier, and he's feeling the heat to bring Jay Plankton back safe and sound to his fans and ex-wives within a matter of hours or preferably minutes. So there's no getting around that that'll be my job twenty-four–seven until Plankton is freed."

"It's almost like the FFF kidnapped Giuliani himself, or Pataki, or George Steinbrenner."

"You got it."

"I'm sure Dave understands your situation, what with his being an officer who aspires to the police detective's life."

"Yeah, Dave says he wouldn't mind working this case himself just to test his oath and his loyalty to the department. He thinks that any grief that falls Jay Plankton's way is just what the bastard has coming. And Dave wasn't sure how hard he'd work to save Plankton from being tortured, at least psychologically. Dave regards Plankton's radio show as a form of psychological torture."

"As do so many of us. But for most of us, our work does not require constant exposure to the J-Bird and his rants."

"Dave once told me that having the J-Bird show on in the squad room every morning is like a scene in some book he read in high school where the government stuffed a guy's head into a small cage and let a hungry rat loose in it. Or threatened to, anyway."

"That's Orwell's *1984*. Dave's is a pretty extreme reaction. Plankton seems to me more gnatlike than ratlike. But anyway I can just choose not to listen."

"For me," Barner said, "torture is having to listen to hip-hop."

"I agree we're a long way from when the cultural heroes of the country's black underclass—and hip middle class—were Ellington and Basie. But the culture as a whole is cruder and meaner. Black people have no monopoly on that."

"Maybe that's what the kidnappers are doing to Plankton right now—making him listen to hip-hop," Barner said.

"For Plankton, that would certainly fit the description of 'feeling the pain,' what the kidnappers said they had in store for the J-Bird."

"Although," Barner said, "if it's Plankton's homophobia that the FFFers are mad about, they probably have some gay-something they're using to get under Plankton's skin."

"Right. Like the tattoos Moyle got. But something that won't just insult Plankton but . . . 'educate' him was what they told Moyle. Moyle was uneducable, the FFFers said, but Plankton, a better candidate for some reason, was headed for the reeducation farm. I don't know what the FFFers have in mind, but the term is ominous. Maoists used it in China and Cambodia."

"Aren't the Amish sort of communistic?" Barner said.

Back to Thad. "No, I don't think so, Lyle. Well, yes, in the sense that there's a theory of sharing, and nonconformity is discouraged. But I don't think the Amish rough people up when they stray from the Mennonite party line. They just treat them like they don't exist. Whoever's got Jay Plankton isn't shunning him. They seem to want him to suffer and to change through suffering."

"Maybe that's not Amish," Barner said, "but it does sound religious. Mennonite is, like, a religion, isn't it?"

"Yes, it's a Christian church, though I think the Mennonites believe in simplicity and self-abnegation, but not self-flagellation."

"I guess Thaddie doesn't have to self-flagellate," Barner said. "Not with you and Timothy Callahan around."

I decided not to try to sort that one out. Instead, I turned up the radio, which described traffic conditions—"flowing smoothly" was the overly optimistic description—as well as the weather. The forecaster said clouding up, then rain early Sunday. This was followed by another report on the abduction of the J-Bird. Little new information was offered, just the release of a statement from the Bush campaign saying the Texas governor had been shocked and saddened by "this attack on a great American," and the entire campaign was praying for Plankton's safe return to his loved ones.

I said to Barner, "There's no relief for the deity's listening posts tonight."

"The pols are keepin' the Almighty hoppin'," he muttered, and hung a right onto Union Avenue.

CHAPTER 18

"So how'd they get away?" Barner was asking two cops, a buxom black woman and her portly white male companion, both of whom appeared to be in their twenties.

"We think they must have come out when the Mister Softee truck stopped in front of the building," the female officer said. "There was a lot of people on the sidewalk waiting for the ice-cream wagon. And then when it stopped, it played its dumb little tune, and more people came out of the bodega across the street where we were parked."

"It was either we didn't spot them come out and walk away through the crowd," the male patrolman said, "or they remained concealed on the other side of the truck."

"This was just, like, five minutes ago," the female officer said. "Jeez, I guess we blew it."

"Jeez, I guess you did," Barner said, and shook his head. The two cops looked glum, hurt and worried.

It was the building superintendent, Ignacio Melendez, in fact, who had informed us upon our arrival that the occupants of Samuel Day's apartment had left the building just minutes earlier. Three men from the apartment had passed by the open door to the super's first-floor apartment. He knew they were under police surveillance, Melendez said, but he did not try to stop them. He assumed the police would follow them. Anyway, he said, he thought the three men might be dangerous if the cops were interested in them. One of the men, according to Melendez, was carrying a long-handled shovel with a sharp blade.

Barner asked the super to describe the men. The one he knew was Sam Day, he said, a tall, bearded man in his forties, who had been renting a second-floor apartment for the past two years. The second man was a slender, paler man of about the same age, with a patch of chin whiskers. He was the one wielding the shovel. Melendez said this man seemed to live with Day at least part of the time, and both of them kept late hours. Their companion when they left the building moments earlier was described as a blue-eyed man with big ears. That sounded like Thad.

The super was lingering in the entryway to the building, along with a number of tenants and neighborhood residents apparently curious about the police presence. They seemed wary but not hostile. Most looked Hispanic. Barner had told me earlier that Williamsburg had become in recent years a mix of Central Americans, Hasidic Jews and hip white kids in their twenties who couldn't afford to live in the no-longer-low-rent East Village near the bars and clubs where they hung out. Most of the young crowd were farther west, though, and the business signs on Lorimer were mainly in Spanish.

Barner and I went up to the super and Lyle asked him to step inside for a moment so they could have a word. In the dingy entryway, Lyle told Melendez, "We'd like to look inside Day's apartment. Have you got a key on you?"

Melendez, round and solid-looking in gray work pants and matching shirt, seemed doubtful. "I don't know. I want to help you out. But don't you got to have a warrant?"

"There's been a kidnapping," Barner said somberly, with just a hint of indignation and even menace. "A man's life may be at stake. Every minute counts. In a life-or-death situation, no warrant is required."

"Is that the radio guy?" Melendez asked.

"Yeah, Jay Plankton."

"You think they got this Plankton guy up on two?"

"Possibly. We have to check it out. If he's in there, he may be injured."

"I never heard no screams."

Barner glanced at his watch and said, "Who owns the building?"

Whoever it was, Melendez looked as if he didn't want to get his employer involved. "Come on," he said, and led us up a narrow stairwell and along a dim hallway to the rear of the building.

Melendez inserted a key from his jingling ring into the lock at 2R, and then a second key into a second lock. The wooden door swung open to reveal not a kidnapper's torture chamber but merely a messy small apartment. As we edged into the living room, where a table lamp was lit, I could hear Timothy Callahan's voice in the far distance: "Surely gay people don't live here."

A daybed in the living room was unmade, and clothes had been tossed over a nearby chair. They looked like Thad's. There were a couple of easy chairs and a coffee table against the wall with an old Zenith TV set atop it with wire-coat-hanger rabbit ears. I stuck my head into the small kitchen. The dishes in the drying rack were clean, and there was a smell of rice-beans-meat takeout coming from the garbage can under the sink.

"That's the bedroom in there," Melendez said.

"Just one?" Barner asked.

"The back apartments, they just got one bedroom."

"Police!" Barner said loudly, and went through the open door. These theatrics were unnecessary, for no one was in the room. The double bed was unmade and more clothes were stacked on makeshift shelves. Barner checked the closet; the clothes inside were neater, hung on hangers above two pieces of luggage. A rear window with a sliding screen stretched into it was open to the warm night air. Outside was a small yard with a single scraggly tree of an unidentifiable type twenty feet below.

Barner opened the suitcases in the closet—empty; no dismembered J-Bird body parts—and checked for name tags, but there weren't any. I went back to the living room. There were magazines and newspapers scattered around— the *New York Press*, the *Village Voice*, the *Nation*, the *New York Review of Books*—and a shelf packed with mostly softcover books. It was an assortment of fairly literate stuff, fiction and nonfiction, with an emphasis on naturalist writing: Peter Matthiessen, Bill McKibben, Roger Tory Peterson. There were gardening books too and tomes on agriculture around the world. You could never be sure ("Katie, they just seemed like the nicest young men until the body parts started showing up in my gladiola bed"), but this looked like the reading material of rational people, not political-radical kidnappers.

When Barner came out of the bedroom, I said, "Maybe they had a shovel because they're farmers. They've got all these books on growing things."

"Not in Brooklyn," Barner said.

"Didn't Walt Whitman grow things here?"

"Not lately."

"Anyway, I think his rural life was farther out on Long Island."

Barner said, "Maybe Day's is, too. There's still some farmland left way east in Suffolk County. They may have gone out there in Diefendorfer's truck." The female officer had gone off to check on Thad's pickup truck, which she said had been parked on the street two blocks away.

I said, "Midnight, Saturday, however, seems like an odd time for farmwork."

"I thought of that," Barner said. "It could be they brought the shovel along for something else. Some bad purpose besides agriculture."

"Could be."

Barner looked through some papers stacked on the back of the kitchen table that was against one wall of the living room, and I watched. "No FFF stuff," I said. "No drafts of ransom notes."

"No."

"It doesn't look like anybody's been held captive here, either."

"Uh-uh."

"This all looks unpromising, Lyle."

"They could still be involved. They could have Plankton out on the Island somewhere. Anyway, Strachey, have you got any better ideas?"

"No, I don't. But so what? You had me a little worried there for a while, Lyle, but there is absolutely nothing in this apartment to suggest that Day or Diefendorfer or the other guy are involved in the kidnapping, or the neo-FFF-anything-else of a criminal nature. And that stuff Leo Moyle said about his captors calling him a sinner and an unrighteous man—maybe it's some Jerry Falwell type we should be looking for. Anyway, my guess at this point is that there's an innocent explanation for Thad meeting up with his old FFF boyfriend and not telling me about it. But it's late, and I'm not about to hang around here and find out tonight. Thad has the number of where I'll be staying, at a friend's place on West Seventy-seventh Street, and I'll leave a note here asking him to call me in the morning. Then we'll know."

Barner gave me a look that I guessed was meant to be incredulous, but it looked forced. He was letting his biases fill the void of no evidence, and I guessed he knew it.

"I'm hoping I'll know what the story is well before morning," Barner said. "I'm going to wait around here until they come back. If they do."

"Good luck."

"You can take the train back to Manhattan. You can get the L at the Lorimer Street station."

"Fine."

The female cop came into the apartment and said, "The pickup's still there. They didn't take it."

Barner screwed up his face, as if this news might indicate something treacherous. "Keep the truck under surveillance," he said. "I'm going to look around here some more."

Melendez the super was in the doorway and stood aside as the young cop went out. He said to Barner, "You gonna stay in the apartment?"

"Yeah. I'll take responsibility."

Melendez looked doubtful. "The radio guy isn't up here."

"Not at the moment," Barner said, making clear with his look that that was the end of that discussion.

The super stood for a moment longer, then turned and went out.

I said, "Isn't what you're doing illegal, Lyle? There's no life-or-death question now."

"You don't know that. You don't know that at all. Plankton is being held by some very rough people who have vowed to hurt him. So, is there a life-or-death issue? I'd say there is."

"In Sam Day's apartment? Where's the evidence?"

Barner closed his eyes, then opened them. "Strachey, do I have to explain this to you, of all people? You know, when you've been doing this as long as I have, you get a feel for these things."

"You're full of it, Lyle," I said, "and you know it, too." I gave him the number of where I'd be staying, wrote out a note asking Thad to call me no matter what time it was, and left Barner fiddling around with a bookshelf, as if it might slide away revealing a secret passageway.

I went out into the wet night air. It was after midnight, and yet the Brooklyn streets were teeming: couples of all ages, mostly straight; young Spanish guys in threes; club kids just heading out; entire large Latino extended families ambling home after some get-together in a restaurant or a relative's apartment. It occurred to me that this echt-urban scene was at least superficially the antithesis of Lancaster County Amish life, and I wondered what Thad and Sam Day, or Dazenfeffer, made of it.

On the platform of the Lorimer L-train station, I waited with a mostly young crowd that was sparse at first, then seemed to grow exponentially. When the Manhattan-bound train finally pulled in four or five minutes later, a Tokyo-sized mob stuffed itself into the six or eight cars. I boarded the final car, where it felt like a party was already under way. The guys were cool in their tight pants and shirts, and the young women were simultaneously glammed up and glammed down in their makeup and party dresses and gray sneakers. It was Lana Turner and Rita Hayworth headed for Ciro's and the Mocambo in sensible shoes. It was no life I had ever known—I had gone almost directly from New Brunswick to Saigon—and it all felt vaguely alien. Yet the unostentatious ease with which these happy kids cast off for a night of partying in the center of the known universe— i.e., the slice of Manhattan bordered by Fourteenth Street on the north and Canal Street on the south—made them seem neither unduly privileged nor in any way depraved. They seemed both wholesome and lucky to be living in America at the pinnacle of its most recent age of innocence.

I was relaxing for a moment and enjoying watching the kids on the party car when my attention was suddenly riveted on the platform across the way. A Canarsie-bound train had just pulled out ahead of ours, and as our train to Manhattan lurched and picked up speed, I was amazed to see a familiar figure hurrying toward the stairs of the Lorimer Street exit. What was Charm Stankewitz doing in Brooklyn, in Williamsburg, in old-FFFer Sam Day's neighborhood?

Reminding myself that Brooklyn was a big place and a lot of people went there for many reasons, I nonetheless exited the train at Bedford Avenue, crossed to the opposite platform, and boarded the next train back to Lorimer. Making my way quickly back to Sam Day's apartment, I watched for Charm on the busy streets, but I didn't spot her. In the subway station, she had been wearing an orange tank top and a red skirt. Slight as she was, I was sure she would stand out in a crowd in that getup. But ten or twelve minutes had gone by, and Charm was nowhere to be seen on Lorimer Street.

The chubby young male cop was standing in the doorway to Sam Day's building. "Is Detective Barner still up there?" I asked.

"Yeah, go on up."

"I don't need to. Did a young woman go in who was wearing a red skirt and skimpy orange top?"

"No, nobody went in."

"Did you notice a young woman fitting that description stop here at all, or just go by?"

The cop thought about this. "Not that I noticed."

"Thanks."

I walked to the end of the block, peered around, then backtracked to the subway. I waited for a time at the top of the station stairs on Lorimer, hoping I might spot Charm, or

Thad and his companions. Or—though I could make no sense of this one—all of them together. But I saw no familiar faces at all, and after several minutes I descended into the overheated tunnel and rejoined the Manhattan-bound stream of party-goers.

During the ride, I struggled to recall Kurt Zinsser's boyfriend Darren's description of Charm's Brooklyn friends that Darren said she visited once a week. There had been no last names given, just one first name, a second first name—Sharon?—and, more memorably, somebody referred to as Strawberry Swirl. I figured I could find a phone book, but it seemed unlikely that I would come upon a listing for "Swirl, S." and a Brooklyn street address.

My ears popped as the train hurtled westward under the East River, and I thought of Leo Moyle's underground transits, one going and one coming back, during his twenty-four hours of captivity. His ears had popped too, he had told Barner, indicating transit via tunnel to Brooklyn, Queens, or New Jersey. Who among all the people I knew with FFF connections were bridge-and-tunnel people? Just Sam Day, plus Charm's Brooklyn friends. Simple coincidence? Could be. Lots of Manhattan-loving nonrich young people actually lived in the once hopelessly unfashionable outer boroughs now. And no connections between any of the assorted known FFF cast of characters made any sense I could begin to imagine. I was missing something, or just way off the beam. Beam me up, Thaddie, I thought—if, unlikely as it seemed, Thad really did know more than he was telling me—Thaddie, beam me up.

I got off the train at the Fourteenth Street–Seventh Avenue station and made my way along the pedestrian tunnel to the platform for the 1 and 9 trains heading up the West Side. This Manhattan station was even hotter than the Brooklyn stations, and it stank of something, too—something pungent that was both off-putting and at the same time had vaguely pleasant associations.

What was it? Not diesel fumes. Years earlier, when I quit smoking, I had loved standing behind buses as they pulled away and sucking up the carbon monoxide fumes they belched into city streets. It was both sickening and at the same time the source of a swell little high of a type I had lost forever.

The stench on the 1 and 9 platform was like that, but both sharper and more indoorsy. What was it? It smelled somewhat medicinal, a bit like cleaning fluid. Oven cleaner? This was Timmy's household-chore-cum-martyrdom, and I knew the smell only from distant corners of our Albany house.

I turned to the bench that was behind me against the station's old worn tile wall, and the odor was even stronger back there. I noticed a small pool of fluid on the wooden bench and an open vial on its side. A popper, that's what it was, that must have fallen out of someone's pocket or backpack. Amyl nitrite—heart medicine originally, and in recent decades a drug inhaled by some gay men, like Lyle Barner's friend Dave and his buddies, to heighten sexual excitement. It hit me that poppers smelled not just hospitallike but also a lot like—where had I just heard someone complaining about the smell?—nail polish.

CHAPTER 19

It was almost 1:30 by the time I climbed the stairs to Broadway and Seventy-ninth into a steady warm rain shower. It hadn't been raining in Brooklyn, but meteorologically New York was a vast continent, and I had moved underground from the Côte d'Ivoire to Ethiopia.

Rainwear or an umbrella would have been nice, but haste was going to have to do. Where were the Bumbershoot people when you needed them most? Whenever Timmy and I had visited European cities in warm weather—Amsterdam, Paris, Florence—we had marveled at the way in which, whenever rain began to fall, tall Africans suddenly materialized selling umbrellas. We had concluded that the umbrella merchants were all members of a West African tribe called the Bumbershoot people. But either the Bumbershoots had not yet made it to New York, or Giuliani had had them all rounded up and shipped back to Europe.

Most of the Upper West Side coffee shops and Chinese and Greek restaurants were shut down by now, but the bars were still open, and there were still plenty of people on Broadway hurrying home or to whatever or whoever was next on their Saturday night dance cards. Just below Seventy-seventh, Big Nick's burger joint, open twenty-four hours, was lively, with people at tables out on the sidewalk under the scaffolding of a building that had been under renovation since early in the Abe Beame administration.

I found an open newsstand and picked up an early-edition Sunday *Times*, a *News* and a *Post*. Plankton's kidnapping was front-page but below the fold in the *Times—Jay Plankton Abducted Outside Apartment*—and full-page on the fronts of both the *News—Plankton Kidnapped*—and the *Post—Gay Radicals Snatch J-Bird*.

I seated myself at a scuffed plastic table under the scaffolding at Nick's, the Upper West Side version of a café on the Champs-Elysées, and ordered black coffee from the harried middle-aged waitress, who looked Cambodian. I ordered the coffee because I had realized back on the platform of the Fourteenth and Seventh subway station that I was going to be up for a while, probably all night and into the next day. I wanted a shower first, and to make some phone calls, but I expected to be back in Brooklyn before the night was through, and then even farther out on Long Island.

While I worked at Nick's coffee, I read the news accounts of the two kidnappings and of Leo Moyle's release. Both the *News* and the *Post* had front-paged the "I ♥ Ricky Martin" and "Kiss Me, Elton" tattoo pix, while the *Times* had chosen to forgo the lurid graphics and let a file photo of Plankton suffice. In the picture he looked far from wholesome, not a figure any self-respecting kidnapper would want to lay hands on, it seemed to me.

The stories on the abductions and Moyle's release were straightforward accounts from police sources and from those few eyewitnesses to the events Saturday afternoon outside the J-Bird's apartment. The FFF figured in all the stories, but the police said they could not be sure that the few vague but ominous communications they had received from the supposed kidnappers were legitimate.

Leo Moyle, all three papers said, remained under police protection in his East Side apartment and had not made himself available to reporters. Jerry Jeris, speaking for Moyle, said that Moyle had weathered his captivity "as well as could be expected," that he was praying for the safe release of his friend, and that he would be filling in for the J-Bird on his show, starting Monday at 6 AM.

The rain was coming down steadier now, but I needed to get moving. Using the bulky classified section of the *Times* as an umbrella, I headed west on Seventy-seventh and let myself into one of the older, well-kept brick apartment buildings interspersed among the brownstones on the leafy block just east of Riverside. Two friends, Susan and Liza, who lived in the building, let me keep not only a set of spare keys but a toothbrush and a change of clothes in a closet near their foldout couch.

Susan and Liza designed outdoor display lighting for tall buildings, and they were frequently in Jakarta or Kuala Lumpur. In New York, one of their jobs was choosing and installing the colored lights used on special occasions in the tower atop the Empire State Building. Both were in Salisbury, Connecticut, for two weeks, lighting a new Indian casino's full-scale replica of a Las Vegas reduced-scale replica of the Eiffel Tower—the developer had made it clear that he didn't want the Parisian tower, but "the Vegas one"—so I had the apartment to myself.

It was just before two when I undressed, turned on the shower, and switched on the radio in the bathroom to the WINS all-news station. The traffic and weather reports had shifted to "moderate" and "warm with showers," and the J-Bird report had changed too, but not for the better.

The news announcer said, "Police have stepped up their efforts to locate Jay Plankton, the talk-radio personality who was abducted Saturday afternoon. Rescuing Plankton turned even more urgent tonight when a package was dropped off at the newsroom of the *New York Post*. Inside the package was a note and an object in a refrigerator bag. The note claimed that the object was Jay Plankton's tongue.

"The note also said that since Plankton had convinced the kidnappers that he could never be 'reeducated,' in their words, he would have to pay an even heavier price. The next piece of Plankton to be sent out would be 'an even more important part of him,' the note said. It was signed by the FFF, or Forces of Free Faggotry, the radical gay group that had been harassing Plankton.

"Police were not certain that the package was sent by the real kidnappers, or if the object inside was an actual human tongue. The package and its contents are being analyzed, a police spokesman said, and NYPD is taking the threat very seriously."

Next was an update on negotiations over an upcoming Bush-Gore debate, but I didn't hang around to listen to it. I postponed the shower, dressed again, found Barner's cellphone number, sat at Susan and Liza's desk, and dialed.

"Barner."

"It's Strachey. I heard."

"This is bad."

"Does it look legit?"

"They think so at the precinct. The tongue thing's at the lab."

"Are you still in Brooklyn?"

"For now. The assholes aren't back yet. I'd have every cop on Long Island looking for them if I knew what they were driving. Diefendorfer's truck is still here, and no vehicle is registered to a Samuel Day in the state of New York."

I said, "I'm coming back out there. I think I know who's got Plankton. It's not Day or Thad or any of them."

"Oh yeah? Then who is it?"

"Lyle, you don't want to know."

"Gotcha. I do but I don't."

"It's Dave."

"Dave who?" It was as if he hadn't heard me.

"Dave Welch, your beau."

"That's bullshit." But he hesitated just perceptibly before he said it.

"I'll explain when I get out there. I'm coming out. Can you get me a ride?"

There was a silence, and then Barner said, "Have you had a couple of drinks, or what?"

"No, just get me over to Williamsburg, and you'll see."

"You're crazy, Strachey. You're nuts."

"Uh-uh. I can explain it. You're smitten with this guy, but you're smarter than you are smitten, and you'll get it. You're not always a smart gay man, Lyle, but you're a smart cop, and that's the Lyle Barner who will see it right away."

"This is nuts. *You're* nuts."

"Can you send a patrol car for me? I'm on the Upper West Side." I gave him the address.

He said, "No."

"No what? You won't even get me a ride?"

"Nah. Uh-uh."

"What if they saw Plankton's dick off? It looks like that's where these dementos are headed next. Do Dave and his pals get high? What do they use? They couldn't be commiting atrocities like this stone cold sober. What all do you know about Dave Welch that you haven't told me, Lyle?"

The line went dead. Barner had hung up.

CHAPTER 20

I caught a cab at Broadway and Seventy-second, and the cabbie, Ahmed something, was willing to take me to Brooklyn. We sped crosstown toward the FDR and the East River bridges. The cab's suspension seemed to fall out at Seventy-second and Third, but Ahmed exhibited no concern over what had happened, so neither did I.

I brought along the cellphone I kept stashed at Susan and Liza's. I had another one I kept in my desk drawer in Albany, and a couple of others in strategic locations. I did not like the things. Nobody who carried them around had enough privacy. You couldn't just bask in your immediate natural surroundings without fear of interruption from afar, or have any kind of uninterfered-with interior life.

Timmy considered my "cellphone phobia" both neurotic and impractical for anyone in my line of work, and I had to agree with him on the last point. Also, as he had explained to me more than once, you can just shut the damn things off. Nor was it required of cellphone owners that they make blabby spectacles of themselves in public places like restaurants, airports and trains. You could own one and still use it considerately. Logic was on Timmy's side, and I knew it was only a matter of time before I was transmittered- and antenna-ed up, if not 24/7/365, then maybe 18/5/312. Still—irrationally, sentimentally, uselessly—I longed for a return to the days when public telephones were black things hung inside stand-up boxes with doors that accordioned shut and that reeked of stale cigarette smoke and Audrey Totter's perfume. And, like Marlowe in *The Big Sleep*, you could pop a nickel in a slot and turn a rotary dial. And then while you waited for whatever bad news or treachery was at the other end of the line, you could sooth your apprehensions by listening to a series of exquisite, subtly mechanical clicks followed by a string of perfectly rolled *R*s that could have been created by the tongue of a Catalonian countess or a sloe-eyed bullfighter.

I brought the cellphone along, even switched it on. Not that I was likely to divulge the number to anyone but Lyle and risk having the thing start twittering next to my pancreas. Of course I would give Thad the number, once I was satisfied, as I was sure I soon would be, that he was not a liar and a kidnapper and a seriously unrighteous, duplicitous Mennonite.

Traffic was lighter than it had been earlier, but even at a quarter to three in the morning the city's main roads felt like workday rush hour in Milan. New York was not just a city that never slept; its nighttime existence constituted a kind of parallel universe to its regular-hours self, and being in that New York night world always felt to me like exciting world travel, like going to Barcelona or Cairo.

The cab rolled up to the Lorimer Street apartment at

3:10 AM. The street was much quieter now, with no sign of the cops who had been watching the building earlier, or of their patrol car. The rain had let up, and the air was fresher in the lungs than it had been, with just an undertone of steamed asphalt and the variegated human smells of the city.

I paid the cabbie, and was turning toward the building when three young people came up the street. One of them said to me in a sarcastic tone, "Hi, schmuck."

"Hey, Charm, it's you. Did you escape from Sing-Sing?"

"I'm not *in* Sing-Sing yet—no thanks to you, asshole."

"What brings you to Brooklyn, Charm? Are you making a woolly cheese delivery to the Williamsburg Incas?"

As her two companions, one male and one female, stood at attention on either side of her glaring at me, Charm snapped, "I'm lucky to be here at all, what with you siccing the staties on me. They told me not to leave Massachusetts, as a matter of fact, but I talked to my dad's lawyer, Graham Witherspoon in Great Barrington, and he says nobody can connect me with any kidnapping, and I haven't been charged with anything, and those goons can *ask* me to do what they want me to do, but they can't *tell* me what to do."

"Uh-huh. But don't you want to be helpful, Charm? The cops just want to find the kidnappers and make sure Jay Plankton is freed before he is maimed any more than he already has been, or even killed."

"What do you mean, maimed?"

She evidently had not heard the news. So I explained about the tongue that had been dropped off earlier at the *Post.* "Or," I asked, "did you send the tongue, and this is another one of your bad-taste stunts in the name of the FFF?"

Charm made a face, and shot back, "Bad taste is only bad taste, so don't start in on that shit with me. Bad taste is in no way comparable to injury or murder. Name one major religion or secular philosophical or ethical construct where taste and morality intersect in any important way. You can't, can you?"

"Oh, Charm, Charm—I think you were not raised Presbyterian."

"No, but I've studied Calvinism, and I think I know the difference between predestination and simple, ephemeral notions of fashion and propriety." Charm's friends, her characteristic claque of two, gazed at her with awe.

"So, are you going in?" I asked, indicating the entrance to Sam Day's building.

"No, why should I go in there?"

"You don't know anyone who lives in here?"

"No, and anyhow we're not going *in* anywhere, we're going *out*."

Charm introduced me to her friends, Louis Murphy and Strawberry Swirl, who lived nearby, and said they were going over to North Sixth Street to the Pussy Pound. Strawberry Swirl, it turned out, was female—lithe and catlike, with no hint of an out-of-control Sealtest–ice-cream habit, despite her name—but Louis was a hulking male and an unlikely habitué of the venue named. Although, I guessed, maybe selected male aficionados were let in too.

I was about to make careful inquiries about what an evening at the Pussy Pound might consist of, and to try to determine if, as it appeared, Charm's showing up on Lorimer Street was coincidental with Sam Day's living there. But before I could do either, Thad Diefendorfer came down the street with two other men.

"Don! Hey, it's you!" Thad recognized me but didn't seem to know Charm, Louis or Strawberry Swirl, and they showed no sign of recognizing Thad or the men on either side of him. "What are you doing out here?" Thad asked. He was holding a long-handled shovel with a sharp, narrow blade.

"I was hoping to talk to you," I said. "I was here earlier,

but I guess you were out . . . what? Practicing a little urban agriculture?"

"Yes," Thad said, "we were over at the Bushwick Community Garden weeding the arugula and watering the tomatoes. The guys both work til ten o'clock, and anyway they like to garden when it's quiet and cool. Don, I want you to meet two friends. This is Daryl Kemmerer, an old friend from Ephrata, and Sam Day. I think I mentioned Sam, my main squeeze back in my FFF days. Now Sam and Daryl are together. Amazing, isn't it? Or not so amazing, really, since Sam was always turned on by simple Amish boys, and there are only a certain number of us available outside of Lancaster County."

There were introductions all around, including Charm, Louis and Strawberry.

"Are you Charm from the cheese farm?" Day asked. He was tall and bearded and wore a sweaty T-shirt with a picture on it of what looked like a head of cabbage. Kemmerer, similarly clad, was lankier, like Thad, with the same big ears that stuck out, chin whiskers, a formidable Adam's apple, and wavy locks that came down the back of his neck.

Charm said, "It looks like I'm famous—Charm from the cheese farm. Cheesy Charm. Oh, right." She gave me the evil eye.

"Well, you sure did a good job of making the FFF look bad," Day said. "Aren't you the one who sent Plankton all the threats and that other weird stuff?"

"The FFF did an awful lot of really good work in its early days," Thad added. "It's really a shame, Charm, that your impression of the organization came strictly from Kurt Zinsser. Kurt was always prickly and a bit uppity, and he doesn't appear to have improved in either regard."

Charm chose not to reply to any of this. She just looked at Day and said, "I've heard of rice queens, and I've heard of dinge queens. And I've heard of snow queens for the dinge queens. But I've never before run into gay men who go for Amish guys. What do you call yourself, Sam, a clip-clop queen? Do you have to worry about getting into masochistic relationships where you start to feel buggy-whipped? Or is that what you're looking for?"

"No," Day said cheerfully. "The two Amish men in my life have been in no way abusive. They've been rational, sweet-natured, gentle and very comfortably masculine."

"Oh, swell, congratulations," Charm said. "And now you're having this rational, gentle, masculine, wild three-some. Can we all come up and watch?"

Kemmerer blushed, Day smiled, and Thad just shook his head. There was a part of me that wanted to compliment Charm on the first intriguing suggestion, however unrealistic it was, that I had ever heard her make. Instead, I said, "I was hoping you'd invite us along to go dancing, or whatever, at the Pussy Pound, Charm."

"Don't you wish," she said, then had to laugh, and the rest of us did, too.

Thad said to me, "How did you find me out here, any-way? Did I tell you where I was staying?"

"No," I said, "but why don't we go on inside, and all that will soon become clear."

"I hope you don't mind if we don't join you," Charm said. "Sitting around with four middle-aged male homosex-uals is not my idea of Saturday night in New York."

We all made it clear that Charm, Louis and Strawberry Swirl would incur no social penalty by moving on, which they soon did.

"So," Thad said, "Charm and her gang are in the all-clear?"

"I'd say so, yes—that is, if they aren't out here conspiring with you three in the kidnappings of Moyle and Plankton."

"Conspiring with us?" Kemmerer said, looking bewil-dered.

"Where would anybody get that idea?" Day said.

Thad smiled wanly and said to me, "Lyle Barner?"

I nodded. "He's inside, in Sam's apartment. He's going to ask you a lot of stupid questions, which you're probably going to have to answer."

"Lyle Barner, the cop?" Day said. "He's in *my* apartment?"

"The super let him in. Don't be too hard on the guy. Lyle made it look legal. Hard to resist, anyway."

I explained to the three of them that Barner had had Thad followed to Brooklyn from Albany, based on nothing more than Thad's FFF history and an irrational antipathy fed by baseless sexual jealousy. And that when Barner discovered that Sam Day, another old FFFer, was the listed tenant of the apartment Thad was visiting, this—plus some as yet unexplained peculiar language that one of the kidnappers used—was all Barner needed to send the kidnapping investigation wackily Thad's way.

"And then," I said, "when he heard you'd left the apartment with a shovel, it seemed to confirm Lyle's worst suspicions."

"Suspicions of what?" Day asked. "Agriculture?"

"It never made sense to me either," I said. "Anyway, I think I know who's got Plankton. It's someone Barner doesn't want to believe would do such a thing, so he may need to abuse the three of you uselessly for a short time before he confronts the obvious. But there's not a lot of time to waste." I described the latest news reports about Jay Plankton's tongue having turned up in the *Post* newsroom.

Thad said, "I'm surprised. I figured these guys to be jokers. Like tattooing Leo Moyle and then letting him go. But this is . . . how could anybody do something that vicious just because the guy was some jerk on the radio?"

Kemmerer said, "How would anybody even know *how* to cut somebody's tongue out?"

"Yes," Day said, "I would expect that to be a lost art on Long Island."

But in fact I had read a month or so earlier about just such a practice. "It's still done by some of the nastier security forces in the Middle East," I said. "You blindfold a man, hold him down, somebody pinches his nose shut, out pops his tongue, and then snip, snip."

They all considered this somberly.

Day said, "So do you think it's Middle Eastern terrorists who have Jay Plankton?"

"No, I think it's some gay cops, high on potent recreational pharmaceuticals, and on resentment and rage. What I have to do now is convince Lyle Barner of this with no hard evidence to go on. But if I can convince him, and if I can get Lyle to accompany me out to his boyfriend Dave Welch's house in Hempstead, I think we can free Jay Plankton before an unavoidable kidnapping and assault charge against the man Lyle loves turns into something even worse."

Day and Kemmerer regarded me with apprehension, and Thad listened thoughtfully, as if he was not altogether convinced. Then Day let us into the building with his key, and the three of them followed me up to Day's apartment on the second floor. The apartment door was locked, and when Day opened it we saw that the lights had been left on, but Lyle Barner was gone.

"Maybe Barner came to the same conclusion you came to, Strachey," Day said, "and he went out to Hempstead to rescue Jay Plankton and arrest his own boyfriend."

Kemmerer said, "Arrest him or warn him," and it occurred to me that Lyle, in the state he must have been in at that moment, might have been capable of either.

CHAPTER 21

Thad had a map of the New York metropolitan area in the glove compartment of his pickup truck, and I navigated as he drove east across Brooklyn and then Queens. A light drizzle was falling again, and Thad drove with determination but care on the slick highways, dodging both potholes, where he could, and early-Sunday-morning drunks.

Day and Kemmerer had offered, without enthusiasm, to ride along and help in any way they could, but that made no sense so they were off the hook. Two of the four of us would have had to ride in the bed of the pickup, either exposed to the weather or under a tarp with eggplant debris. Anyhow, what were they going to do when we arrived at Welch's house, the address of which was conveniently listed in the Nassau County phone book? Thad and I assured Day and

Kemmerer that once we became convinced that Jay Plankton was in fact being held in Hempstead, we would notify the local police department before proceding.

The radio news reports offered no substantive late developments. The headlines were still the tongue arriving at the *Post* and the threat of additional gruesome bodily harm to Plankton. The reporter did add that following Sunday morning services at Saint Patrick's Cathedral, Archbishop Egan was expected to make a personal appeal to the kidnappers for the J-Bird's release. Joining the cleric in his plea would be Babette Gallagher, a woman who described herself as Jay Plankton's "fiancée." Interviewed by WINS, Gallagher spoke with emotion but said in a controlled voice that her boyfriend "did not deserve to be mutilated." She added, "Jay is no saint, but who is?"

Just after 4:30, Thad and I pulled into a Dunkin' Donuts near the West Hempstead Long Island Rail Road station. I went in and asked for directions to Parsons Drive. This produced an elaborate confab involving all of the shift personnel. The consensus was that Parsons Drive was just four blocks away. I bought two black coffees and a bag of crullers, and went back out to the truck.

"It's nearby. Go down that way three blocks, and turn right."

"Then what?" Thad said.

"I don't know."

"When should we call the police?"

I got out my cellphone, switched it on, and told Diefendorfer, "I don't know the answer to that, either. When the time comes, we'll recognize it, I think."

Thad drove out onto the highway. "This is kind of exciting," he said.

"Do you have goose bumps?"

"I think so. But I'm developing a lot of gas, too. I guess I'm not nineteen anymore."

We soon turned off the commercial street onto a leafy

avenue of ample wood-frame and shingled single-family residences with small but tidy lawns and glistening, rain-drenched late-model sedans and SUVs in the driveways. Few lights were on in the houses, but the streetlights at the intersections cast enough illumination for us to read some of the house numbers, and we soon spotted Dave Welch's place.

"Go on by," I told Thad.

"Right. Let's think this through."

Welch's house was a two-story, brown-shingled place with a chalet-style **A** over the front door, a couple of big oaks on either side of the structure, and bushy shrubs under all the first-floor windows. A screened porch on the left side of the house was dark, as were the other first-floor rooms. Up above, though, dim lights were visible behind drawn curtains at two second-story windows. Three cars were parked out front: a gray Toyota Previa and a black VW Passat, one behind the other in the driveway, and a beige Ford sedan on the street. The Ford looked as though it could have been an NYPD unmarked car, maybe Lyle's.

"The Toyota could be the getaway car," I said. "After they grabbed Plankton, they put him in a stolen Lincoln Navigator and then they switched to what one witness thought was a light-colored van. The Previa could be mistaken for a van."

"It's funny that they wouldn't hide it," Thad said.

"It's a vague description that fits a lot of vehicles in the state of New York."

Thad cruised down the block, made a U in an intersection, then slowly backtracked.

"Let's park here," I said, and Thad pulled in front of a darkened house two doors up and across the street from Welch's. We had a clear view of the Welch house. The second-floor lights remained on, but no movement was detectable behind the curtains. Thad doused his headlights and cut the engine. No lights had been on in any of the other nearby houses, and none came on when we parked. If our activities aroused the interest of any neighborhood insomniacs, they were not letting us know it.

"Now what?" Thad said.

"I'm thinking this over."

Thad rolled his window down, and after a moment he said, "I don't hear anything."

"No."

"They'd probably have Plankton gagged. Don't you think?"

"Yes, although if they actually cut out his tongue, I guess he'd be limited in the sounds he could make. Anyway, he would be physically traumatized by that ordeal, and maybe not even conscious."

"That's awful. I sure hope they didn't do it."

The night air was warm, and the cab of Thad's truck smelled of him and of eggplant, both pleasing.

After a time, I said, "Thad, you don't happen to have a firearm with you, do you? In the glove compartment?"

"No, I don't own a gun."

"Mine is in Albany," I said. "I didn't anticipate a confrontation with violent people. At least, not without being in the company of the New York Police Department. By that I mean, being in the company of NYPD officers and with their being on my side in this thing."

"Of course, there's been some ambiguity about which side you're on," Thad said.

"Not really. Not when it comes to bodily harm. I'm against that, generally speaking."

"Oh, good."

"But self-defense might soon become an issue. I take it you have no problem with self-defense."

"I prefer to avoid situations where I might be called upon to employ, say, fisticuffs. On the other hand, if someone is bent on causing me serious bodily injury, I suppose I could find it within my ethical means to eviscerate the poor soul."

"Great."

We sat some more, peering over at the Welch house.

"What I need to know," I said after a moment, "is who is in there, and are they armed? Being cops, chances are they are."

"Right."

"I'm especially interested to know if Lyle is inside that house. And if so, what is his situation vis-à-vis the others inside?"

"Why don't you call him up and ask him?" Thad said. "You have his cellphone number. If he's in there, you don't have to tell him that you're sitting in a truck across the street."

"Hmm."

"Barner might not be willing to tell you where he is at all. Which would be a good indication that he's up to no good and is probably inside Welch's house. Actually, I could go over there and hide in the darkness, and I could listen for a phone to ring inside. It's so quiet around here that I'd probably hear it."

"I don't know," I said. "It's somewhat risky for you, Thad. Can you protect yourself if you have to?"

"I've got a tire iron under the seat. I can take that. But I won't get caught. All my old skulking skills will surely come back. I'll bet skulking is like swimming or riding a bicycle. Your body doesn't forget habitual sneaking around."

"Are you getting goose bumps again?"

"No, I think I'm too exhausted for goose bumps. I haven't been up this late since about 1980. Most farmers are just getting out of bed at this hour, not still up from the night before. But I've got enough adrenaline pumping now to do whatever it is we need to do. The caffeine should help, too," Thad said, and took a swig of his coffee.

"Okay, go ahead. When I've lost sight of you, I'll wait thirty seconds and then dial."

"Make it a minute," Thad said. "Let me get used to the sounds around the house."

"Okay. I'll dial sixty seconds after I've lost sight of you."

Thad reached under his seat, groped around, and soon came up with a tire iron. "Here goes," he said. He switched the cab's overhead light to the off position so the cab would not light up when he opened the door. He exited the truck quietly, then eased the door shut with a soft click.

Thad strode across Parsons Drive as if he belonged there and moved quickly along the sidewalk to Welch's house. He glanced my way once, then cut left into the darkness near the side porch. While I counted to sixty, I watched for lights to come on in the Welch house or in any others, but none did.

When a minute had passed, I retrieved the scrap of paper with Lyle's cellphone number, flipped open the glove-box door for illumination, opened up my phone, and dialed.

Even from where I sat, a hundred or more feet away, I could hear the phone twitter.

It was answered after one ring, and it was unmistakably Lyle who said calmly, "Hey, Strachey, I think your Amish sweetheart is taking a leak in the bushes about ten feet from me. That's not very sanitary, if you ask me. Or very polite."

"Lyle? Is that you?" What was he up to?

"Yeah, it's me. I'm stretched out on a lounge inside the porch you're looking at, having a well-earned refreshment."

"You're on the porch?"

"Yeah, the one you're lookin' at right now from the cab of Diefendorfer's pickup truck. I sat here and watched the two of you sittin' over there smoochin'. Then Thaddie gets out, and he ambles over here by where I'm relaxing. He's done taking a piss, it looks like, and now he's standing close in beside a big bush and I'm looking right at him."

"How did you know it was us?"

"I had a locator beacon placed in the truck. It's under the right front fender."

"I see. When did you do that, Lyle?"

"Three hours ago, back in Brooklyn."

"May I ask why you did that?"

"Two reasons. One is, I still wasn't certain I could trust Diefendorfer. The man is a known liar. The other reason is, I wasn't really sure myself what I was going to find when I arrived out here, and I needed to know if and when you might turn up and complicate my life. You were tracked all the way to Hempstead, and I was given updates every three minutes right up until the time you parked across the street from where I'm sitting. Two patrol cars from the Hempstead Police Department are parked a block and a half from where you are, and those officers are ready to move in on you if I ask them too."

"So then," I said, "Jay Plankton is not being held captive by Dave Welch and his cop friends in Welch's house? Or was Plankton there earlier, but you tipped Welch off and they all got away?"

Barner grunted, or maybe belched lightly. "Nuh-uh. None of the above, you stupid fuck. Why don't you come over here, Strachey, have a beer, and I'll show you around. You can see for yourself, if that's what you need, what's been happening here tonight. It's no kidnapping, that's for sure. It's all voluntary, involving consenting adults. Have a look, and tell your pal there, Thaddie, to come on inside, too. He looks to me like he turned into somebody in a wax museum out there, and he might want to come in and chill out."

Thad had to have heard Lyle's end of this conversation, but apparently he was waiting for some signal from me. Was this a trap of some sort? It didn't feel like one at all. I climbed out of the truck, shut the door, and walked toward the darkened porch, with the phone line to Lyle still open.

"There's a door on the back of the porch," Lyle said. "It's unlocked." Then he hung up.

A light drizzle was still drifting down. The grass in Welch's yard was wet and smelled of ammonia. I was unable to see Thad, but as I neared the porch, I said, "Thad, let's go on in," and he stepped from behind a lilac bush and joined me.

We found the door to the porch, opened it, and stepped inside.

"Welcome to Hempstead, guys," said a voice that wasn't Lyle's.

A match was struck and Dave Welch lit a candle on the table alongside the padded porch chair he was sitting in. Stretched out on a nearby chaise, Lyle was fully dressed, while Welch was clad only in gym shorts.

"Hi," Thad said, "I'm Thaddeus Diefendorfer."

Not getting up, Welch extended his hand. "I'm Dave Welch."

"Pleased to meet you."

"I understand from Lyle that the two of you suspected me of kidnapping and tattooing Leo Moyle, and then kidnapping and mutilating Jay Plankton." Welch swigged from a bottle of Sam Adams.

"That came from me," I said. "Was I totally off base?"

"Yeah," Welch said. "You were totally off base. I despise Plankton and his gang. I have to listen to their stupid crap every morning in the precinct house, and if somebody kicked the shit out of them, I'd hate to have to be the arresting officer. But am I a violent criminal? No, I'm not. I'm a cop."

Thad said, "But aren't cops sometimes violent criminals? I've read of a number of cases. The men who abused and tortured Abner Louima, for example."

"Yeah," Welch said, "this can happen. Psychopathic

personalities slip through, like anywhere else. And any department gets its share of goons and bullies. But I'm not one of either category. It's exactly what I'm against, as a matter of fact."

"I'm glad to hear that," Thad said. "Because it seems to me that police departments shouldn't let any psychopathic personalities slip through. And if they do, they ought to be chucked out. All the goons and bullies, too."

Lyle said sarcastically, "Tell us about it." I had thought he'd been drinking, but he had a can of Coke in his hand and appeared weary but cold sober. Only Welch was drinking, although he was also coherent, even alert.

"If either of you have any doubts about my noninvolvement in the kidnappings," Welch said, "feel free to look around the house. You'll find evidence of a type of partying that Lyle's not crazy about, but nothing that's illegal in the state of New York. Nothing to speak of, anyway. One of the guys smoked a little weed, but that's about it. It's been ten or fifteen years since sodomy's been illegal in the state, so none of us will be doing time in Dannemora on that one."

Thad said, "Were you having a sex party? Lord, I haven't been to one of those for over twenty years. I'm as good as married now, but I harbor fond memories of my orgiastic youth."

"Fond memories!" Lyle spat out. "Jesus Christ!"

I said, "Thad, I take it that this wasn't back in Lancaster County."

"No, New York and San Francisco in my FFF days. You'll find homosexual dalliances among the Amish, like anywhere else, but no group activity, I think. Barn raising never turned into hayloft orgies among the Mennonite farmers that I heard about."

"Please explain," Welch said to me, "what it was besides my dislike of Plankton that made you think I was behind the kidnappings. This is really very weird. Lyle says he never believed you, but my poor bed-buddy here drove all the way out here from the city to—I think—confront me, search the house, and assure himself that I was no sadistic fiend and kidnapper. Now what was that *about?*"

Bed-buddy. What did that mean? Poor Lyle thought of Welch as his lover, or boyfriend.

I said, "First, just to add purity to your generally persuasive denials of complicity, Dave, I'd like to take you up on your offer of allowing us to look around your house. Okay?"

Welch shrugged.

"Thad, why don't you give the place a quick look while I backtrack and try to recall exactly what it was that led us out here in the middle of the night. You're the breaking-and-entering specialist. Do you mind?"

"I'd rather not do that."

"All right."

"If it were a rescue, sure. But if it's an orgy, I don't want to see it and experience temptation. Not that I would necessarily be invited to participate. Don't get me wrong."

"I think Delmar and Marty are asleep," Welch said. "But you would certainly be invited, Thad, if you were interested. That goes for you too, Strachey, despite your coming out here to malign my character."

At that, Lyle got up abruptly and went inside the house. "I can't take this," he said as he left.

After a moment, Welch sighed. "I'm sorry. I love Lyle, but I'm not about to settle in with one guy. I'm too restless. And I want to focus on my career and on reforming the department. Lyle's role models in love are his mother and father, and if any two guys or any two women want that, that's fine. But it's not for me."

"Apparently not," Thad said. "I'll go in and see how Lyle's doing. Maybe you need to just cut him loose. Or maybe he should cut *you* loose, if he can."

Welch did not reply, and Thad went into the house, where a light had come on in a distant inside room.

"Lyle is so upset with me," Welch said to me, "that you almost had him believing I was a major felon."

"And he's so smitten with you that he almost had me believing he was going to tip you off that I was onto you—or even that he was your accomplice."

Welch swigged more beer. "So," he said after a moment, "what made you decide I was a kidnapper?"

I explained how comments Lyle had made about Welch's rage over the J-Bird and his radio show had predisposed me to becoming suspicious of him, and how Lyle's apparently exaggerated remarks about Welch's drug use had fueled that predisposition. Then after Leo Moyle told of the powerful scent of fingernail polish in the room where he had been held, I connected that with Welch's use of poppers, which smelled like nail polish, and Welch and his mysterious cohorts suddenly became the obvious culprits.

"We do use poppers," Welch said. "They're probably not healthy, but they're legal. None of us use fingernail polish, though. Delmar, Marty and I are all police officers, and colored nails would not go over big in the department."

"There was also," I said, "the fact that with Jay Plankton's situation becoming increasingly desperate, some of us hired to find him probably started getting desperate, too. You heard about the tongue at the *Post*, I take it."

"I doubt if that's real," Welch said. "Who would do that? It's too wild, too much."

"I hope so."

"Before you pulled up across the street, Lyle was on the phone with the other detectives working the case, including the feds, and he said everybody was sounding desperate. The forensics weren't in on the tongue yet, and nobody could find a tattoo artist who looked like a good suspect for the Moyle inkwork. There are hundreds of licensed tattoo parlors in the metro area, and nobody knows how many unlicensed amateurs, it turns out. They'd been hoping that the tattoo search would churn something up. And I guess the FFF end of the investigation hasn't been productive either."

"Not so far," I said. "The harassment of Plankton, supposedly by FFFers, was just some angry kids in Massachusetts. And apparently the kidnappers then picked up on the FFF name, hoping the kids would be the prime suspects. But they weren't for long."

With faint light now discernible through the low clouds in the east, Welch and I reviewed the case for several minutes, until Thad and Lyle reappeared. Lyle seemed to have calmed down. To distract him, Thad had asked for a tour of the Welch house, ostensibly to reassure Thad that Jay Plankton was not bound and gagged somewhere. Thad reported to me that it was true—Plankton was nowhere in the house, and there was no evidence that he had ever been there.

"Upstairs there are two hunky naked guys on a big bed," Thad said, "snoring to beat the band. Earlier somebody had spilled a vial of poppers on a pillow, and the place still reeked. It's a powerful aroma, and I can understand, Strachey, why when you smelled the popper in the subway it triggered this really strong reaction on your part, like Marcel Proust's madeleine.

"But this stuff didn't really smell like nail polish. It's sweeter, and not so pungent. I was thinking, there's nothing that smells exactly like nail polish. So maybe what Leo Moyle smelled really *was* nail polish. Wouldn't Moyle and the J-Bird and those guys recognize nail polish when they smelled it? They've got all those girlfriends and ex-wives and ex-girlfriends who probably did their nails a lot. So the J-Bird gang would surely know that smell when they were near it," Thad said.

That's when something I had been dimly aware of since one of my annoying conversations with Jerry Jerris and Jay Plankton in Jeris's office started to come back to me.

CHAPTER 22

I was seated at Dave Welch's kitchen table, and I had Leo Moyle on the phone. On the table in front of me were the few remaining crumbs from the crullers. And instead of joining Welch in a beer, I was back at the takeout coffee, which Welch had zapped in his microwave. This brought out the brew's acidic qualities, which I needed.

A groggy-sounding woman had answered Moyle's telephone. Apparently he had taken Jerry Jeris's advice on how to help regain his mental health. The woman was reluctant to awaken Moyle at daybreak, but when I explained that the information might save Jay Plankton from additional harm, she relented, and Moyle was soon on the line.

I asked him, "What do you know about Steve Glodt's personal life?"

"You woke me up at 5:30 A.M. to ask me *what*?"

"Jerry Jeris and Jay Plankton once mentioned to me in passing that Steve Glodt had a girlfriend in Oyster Bay who runs a nail parlor. It was my impression from this conversation, as I recall it, that Glodt also has a wife wherever he lives on Long Island. Is all of that true? I'll explain in a minute why I'm waking you up at this early hour, and how all this might be relevant to your kidnapping and to Jay's."

There was a pause, and then Moyle said, "What are you trying to say, Strachey? Just spit it the fuck out. What are you implying about Steve?"

"It sounds, Leo, as if you are ready to be indignant over any imputation of wrongdoing on the part of your big boss, Steve Glodt. I guess you are much fonder of Glodt than it's my impression Jerry Jeris and Jay Plankton are. Your confidence in his integrity is far greater than theirs. They both talked about Glodt as if he is greedy, mendacious, treacherous. Maybe your experience with Glodt has been different."

Moyle said, "Steve's a total asshole, don't get me wrong."

"Uh-huh."

"But what are you saying? That Steve had me snatched and dragged out to the Island and tortured? And now he's doing the same thing to Jay? Even if he was that skanky, why would he do that? Sure, Steve is a depraved son of a bitch. Anybody who's ever been in contract negotiations with him knows that. The man is capable of just about anything he thinks he can get away with. But why would he do this to Jay and I? There'd be nothing in it for him."

"What about publicity? A spike in the ratings?"

"The show's ratings have never been higher," Moyle said. "Unless . . ." There was a silence.

"Unless what?"

"Unless Steve thought that by putting Jay and me through the wringer it would make us angrier."

"Why would he want that?"

Moyle was breathing audibly now, as if the idea that someone was calculatedly trying to make him angrier was making him angrier.

"Steve's been working on a deal to get the show simulcast on cable TV—on GSN, the Gonzo Sports Network. But according to Irene Wojkowski, my agent, the GSN people have been offering less money than Steve thinks the deal is worth. They told him they thought the show was losing its edge, that we all weren't angry enough. The angry-white-male audience wants raw red meat, and the GSN people aren't sure we're mean enough. They want us foaming at the mouth for three hours a day, Irene said, and they claim we aren't doing it. Which is idiotic, because Jay and I are as vicious as we've ever been, and if any pussy-whipped dickhead tries to say otherwise to my face, I'll break his pansy-wrISTed fag neck."

Could necks have wrists? Now was not the time to inquire. "I guess, Leo, that when you use the term 'mean,' you are using it in the Jack Welch–style American corporate sense. By 'mean,' you mean relentlessly, even amorally, profit-oriented."

"Not really," Moyle said. "By 'mean,' I mean shitting on wussy, oversensitive, PC types of people for the sheer, sadistic pleasure of it."

"I'm sorry if I impugned your motives."

"Steve Glodt is only interested in money," Moyle said. "I have my beliefs, and I have my principles."

"So tell me about rotten, unprincipled Steve Glodt's girlfriend in Oyster Bay. She runs a nail parlor there?"

"I've heard that, yeah. She has an apartment over the nail parlor, and Steve spends as much time there as he does with his hideous wife in his mansion in Center Island, according to Irene. The wife knows about it, but what's she gonna do? Out in the open market, she'd be worth about eighty-nine cents a pound, and she'd miss her Chris-Craft and her helipad and her New Year's–to–Groundhog Day in Boca. The setup works perfectly for everybody involved."

"What's the girlfriend's name?"

"Annette, I think. But that might not be her real name. No, it is, it's Annette something. Listen," Moyle said, "do you really think Steve could be behind the kidnappings? I've been fucked over by people I knew before, but . . . This could be some major shit of a type that a man even as cynical as I can be finds very hard to get my mind around."

"I'm not sure," I said, "but Glodt is looking more and more promising. The girlfriend's apartment over the nail parlor in Oyster Bay might have been where you were held, and it sounds like a good locale to produce an overwhelming smell of nail polish. It's the right distance from the city too, at the end of a route that includes tunnels and expressways. And now you yourself, need I add, have offered up a specific motive, even beyond Glodt's well-known general horribleness. Is it safe to say that when you do the J-Bird's show on Monday, you'll be seething?"

"Oh, I'll be pissed beyond belief—at Steve, if he did it."

"But even if you went into the studio Monday morning thinking some radical gay group like the FFF was responsible for what happened to you and the J-Bird, you'd be very, very angry, wouldn't you, Leo?"

"I'd be ripshit."

"A state of affairs that would not go unnoticed at GSN, I'll bet."

I described to Moyle the overnight development in the case, where a moist object that the kidnappers asserted was Jay Plankton's tongue had turned up in the *New York Post* newsroom. "But I doubt it's actually the J-Bird's tongue," I said. "Plankton would be of no use to Glodt if the J-Bird was in a perpetual rage every weekday morning but his diction was worse than Quasimodo's."

Moyle said, "If Steve is actually behind this, somebody's tongue is gonna get ripped out, but it's not gonna be Jay's. If Annette wants her cunt licked in the future, she's gonna have to go down to the pet store and shop for a new friend other than Steve Glodt."

I guessed Moyle was speaking figuratively in his colorful way, but his breathing was sounding labored again, so I wasn't sure.

CHAPTER 23

Oyster Bay, despite the popular misconception, was a largely working-class town on the Island's generally silk-stockinged North Shore. Theodore Roosevelt had had a home there—Sagamore Hill, now a museum—but most of the town's residents were neither political nor business aristocracy. They were the people who installed the hot tubs, pumped out the septic tanks, and rolled the lawns of this section of Long Island's old and new rich. Oyster Bay, it appeared, as we drove through it en route to the House of Annette: Nails of Glory—which we had found in the Nassau County yellow pages—was not so much a Jay Gatsby town or a Tom and Daisy Buchanan town as it was a George and Myrtle Wilson town.

There was no Doctor T. J. Eckleburg sign, as in *Gatsby,*

but plenty of suburban retail and office sprawl, most of it identical to what we'd passed in Hempstead. One difference between the commercial suburbia I was familiar with in Albany and that of Oyster Bay was the Long Island preponderance of retail stores in long buildings, probably dating to the 1920s and 1930s and done in a brick "colonial" motif or an "Old English" style that featured leaded windows and exposed timbers. These were the North Shore versions of LA strip malls, except sometimes with second stories.

The strip we parked down the street from included—along with a pizza parlor, a tae kwon do emporium, and a copying center—the House of Annette: Nails of Glory. Of additional interest to Lyle, Dave Welch, Thad, and me—all of us in Lyle's NYPD Ford—was Annette's next-door neighbor, Damien's Den of In-Ink-Kwity, a tattoo parlor.

At 6:25 Sunday morning, all of the businesses were closed. So was the chain video store we were parked in front of. Traffic was all but nonexistent, and a fine mist was in the air, which was so rainforestlike that I would not have been surprised to hear a macaw cackling or see a salamander skitter across the hood of the Ford.

We sat for several minutes going over our options. Both Barner and Welch were skeptical of my theory—which had become a conviction over the past hour—that Steve Glodt was the mastermind behind the Moyle and Plankton kidnappings. Both cops agreed that powerful people were capable of savage criminal acts—Lyle had seen it numberless times over his long career—but they both doubted that Glodt would be so spectacularly arrogant and reckless.

Having spent a couple of days, off and on, with Jeris, Plankton, and Moyle, I thought I understood them well enough to make this argument: Glodt had calculated he had plenty to gain from the cruel stunt—publicity and, even more importantly, added "edge" that the Gonzo Sports Network would go for. And he figured he had little to lose if caught. Glodt could well have speculated that if Plankton and Moyle remained in character, they would consider the whole thing a hilarious practical joke—just guys joshing other guys on a colossal scale—and they would consider it unsporting, even unmanly, to press charges or ever to testify in court against the charmingly roguish prankster who also happened to own their network.

Having observed Plankton and Jeris at their most oafish, Thad found my scenario plausible. He was also eager to expose Glodt and, like me, to test the limits of the J-Bird's willingness to let sadistic straight male jerks of a well-known type be sadistic straight male jerks of a well-known type. Lyle was indulging Thad and me by driving us over to Oyster Bay, and Welch came along to watch. On the way to Oyster Bay, Lyle had checked again with the other detectives working the case back in the city, but none reported any breaks.

Lyle said, "Miss Annette living next door to a tattoo parlor does get my attention."

"Is this one of the tattooists that was checked?" Welch asked.

"I'll find out."

Lyle phoned his office, spoke to someone there, and hung up. "It was checked out yesterday by the Oyster Bay department."

I said, "What did the questioning consist of? Did they ask Damien the tattooist if he was involved in the Moyle kidnapping, and he said no, and they left, or what?"

"It could have been something like that."

We sat for another minute looking down the street through the mist at the nail and tattoo parlors. The long business block was set back from the highway about thirty feet, with face-in parking along the facade. The second-story windows bore no signs or lettering, and it looked as if there were apartments behind them. That would square with my information from the J-Bird gang that Glodt's girlfriend lived above her nail parlor. At the center of the block was what looked like a first-floor entryway leading to the second-floor apartments. Fire regulations, I guessed, would have required a second entrance and stairway, probably in the rear of the building.

Thad said, "What if we just went up to the apartment over the nail parlor and knocked on the door?"

"And say what?" Lyle said. "Even if I identified myself as a police officer, whoever's in there could tell me to screw off. I could wake up a judge and ask for a search warrant if I had something more to go on than Strachey's imagination running wild. But I don't, so getting in there with either a legal document or a battering ram is not in the cards."

"The chances are good," I said, "that at this early hour everybody inside the apartment is asleep. Maybe Thad and I could get inside the apartment, look around, and either confirm that the J-Bird is being held in there or that he isn't, and then leave. Thad, do you think you could get us inside?"

"Probably so. It's an old building without a lot of updating otherwise, so it may well have old locks I could go right through. Do any of you have a lobster pick with you? I reckon not."

Lyle said, "I have a department tool you could use. But I'm just trying to figure out how I'm supposed to explain to a commander—or to a department inspector or to a judge—that the rescue of Jay Plankton was effected through a citizen's breaking and entering—and a B and E that I was myself an accessory to. Or even worse than that—and this is the likeliest way for all this to play out—that Plankton isn't in there at all, but my lockpicker was employed in a B and E that led to a ten-million-dollar lawsuit against the department, against an Albany PI, and against a Mennonite turnip farmer from Jersey."

"Eggplant," Thad said.

"But Lyle has a point." Now this was Welch getting into

it. "If you going in there the way you said goes wrong, we're all fucked. That's why I think, Thad, that instead of you using Lyle's department equipment, you should use some of the finer implements on my Swiss Army knife, which maybe you found on the roadside somewhere. And that while you go in, Lyle and I should cruise up and down the highway until we get a call from you to either pick you up, and we all go to IHOP for breakfast, or to come to your aid pronto and we do."

Lyle was shaking his head, but instead of objecting he just let out a long sigh and said, "Jee-sus."

Thad and I were in the backseat of the Ford, and when Welch reached over the seat to hand Thad the Swiss Army knife, I saw that Thad had goose bumps on his arm. His hand was not trembling, though, an indication that he was anticipating not sex but house-breaking. An unusual Mennonite was Thad, or so I assumed from my limited experience.

Lyle made Thad and me both memorize his cellphone number, and when we had, we climbed out into a fine spray of light rain.

"This feels nice," Thad said. "I feel like a pile of fresh lettuce at the old Rinella's market in Ephrata when I was a kid. They had a machine that sprayed the produce, and I liked to stick my face in the mist."

"Actually, those gadgets are back," I told Thad, as Lyle pulled onto the highway and headed away from the strip mall. "I saw one in a supermarket recently that not only misted the greens periodically, but when it did so a nearby speaker broadcast thunderstorm sounds."

"And let loose with a blast of Ferde Grofé?"

"I'm not kidding," I told him, and I wasn't.

"No lightning bolts though, I hope."

"Not yet."

We crossed the highway and walked toward the business strip with apartments above it, then cut along the side of the building and around back. There we found an acre of tarmac, with garbage dumpsters next to some of the rear entrances to the pizza parlor and the other businesses. Six cars were parked side by side at the far rear of the paved area, which apparently provided parking for the business employees and the building's second-floor tenants. No light-colored van was among the cars, just Chevy, Pontiac and Honda sedans and a beat-up old VW Rabbit.

We noted the location of the nail parlor, the second business from the far end of the building, next to the tattoo den.

Thad said, "What if Miss Annette's apartment is above her nail parlor, but not directly above it? What if we waltz into somebody else's home by mistake?"

"We'll apologize," I said, "and ask where Miss Annette lives."

"Sounds like a plan."

The entrance to the rear stairway was in the center of the building, opposite the one in the front, and Thad had no trouble making his way through the lock in well under thirty seconds.

"You'd make a successful criminal," I told him.

"Thank you. I once was one. Not much of what the FFF did way back when was legal."

At the top of the wooden stairway was a long corridor going off to the left and to the right. Directly ahead was a wider stairway leading down to the front entrance. We turned left, toward the apartment over the nail parlor. There were three doors, however, one apparently to an apartment in the front of the building, one to an apartment in the rear, and one on the far end.

Thad said, "Uh oh."

"It's probably the front one or the rear one," I said.

"Yes, one or the other."

We checked the name cards on the doors. The one on the front apartment said "Gomspold," and the card on the rear apartment said "D. Carletti."

"Could it be Annette Gomspold?" Thad whispered.

"Maybe. And I wonder if the other one is Damien Carletti, the tattooist?"

But when we checked the door at the end of the hallway, the name card read "Annette C. Koontz."

"I smell coffee brewing," Thad said. "But it seems to be coming from Gomspold's place."

These apartments, so close to one another, suddenly struck me as unlikely venues for holding kidnap victims. Even if the captives were bound and gagged and unable to cry for help, as Moyle said had been the case with him, getting them in and out of this building without attracting attention seemed like a stretch. My conviction that Steve Glodt was behind the kidnappings and that the J-Bird was being held, and possibly tortured and mutilated, in Annette Koontz's apartment—assuming that this woman actually had any connection whatever with Glodt—was starting to waver.

Thad said, "I'll just knock on the door lightly to see if anyone is up and about. If there's no response, I'll go in." He had the corkscrew from Dave Welch's Swiss army knife poised.

I thought, What am I doing here? How did I get mixed up in this thing? Why am I not home in bed in Albany with Timothy Callahan, instead of prowling through a building in Oyster Bay, Long Island, probably about to scare the crap out of some innocent workingwoman who is luxuriating in the only rest and solitude she can enjoy all week long? Could I have my PI license revoked for this? Or be convicted of a felony? Would it be house-breaking? Stalking? Invasion and assault?

Thad rapped lightly on Annette Koontz's door.

We waited.

No sound came from the Koontz apartment or from any of the others.

Thad looked at me, but before I could suggest that maybe we should reconsider what now felt like a reckless, even idiotic, misadventure, he had inserted the business end of his implement in the door's single lock, quickly maneuvered it this way and that, and when he turned the knob, the door swung open.

We stood for a moment looking into a living room furnished with some fat leather chairs and a beige leather couch—Had a woman purchased these objects?—and a large-screen TV. It had been set inside one of those home-entertainment-center type structures ("A man's home is his megaplex"), which had a small bar attached to it. The illumination was dim, coming from a double window whose shades were lowered.

Thad looked at me again, then stepped carefully inside the apartment. I followed him. A familiar voice said levelly, "Shut the door, you pond-scum, puke-ass-faggot, maggot-head creeps."

Jay Plankton was holding an automatic weapon the size of a grenade launcher, and it was aimed at Thad and me. He was standing in the semidarkness of a doorway leading to a room in the back of the building. His good diction indicated that he still had his tongue.

Thad said, "Hey, J-Bird, we come as friends."

"Rescuers," I added. "If that's what's needed, here we are."

"Shut the door," he said again, and I did as I was told.

Thad said, "So you're in on it? Way cool."

"You fooled me, Jay," I added. "What a prank! You're . . . you're *too much*, you crazy fucker, you."

"You can cut the showbiz crap," Plankton snapped. "I've reached my limit, and I'm not taking it anymore. No more. No more." He sounded exhausted, desperate.

"Jay, you're cracking me up," I said. "If you put that gun down, I'd collapse on the floor laughing. That is the idea, isn't it?"

But the look in Plankton's eye was not one of devilish merriment, or even of guilt. He looked enraged and crazed.

"You're going to get in there with your friends," he said, moving into the room with us, and waving toward the back room with his revolver. "And then I'm going to decide what to do with you. A good possibility is justifiable homicide."

"What would the justification be?" Thad asked.

"I'm in a bad mood," Plankton shot back. "How's that?"

"Interesting," Thad said, being careful, I guessed, not to worsen Plankton's mood.

I said, "We're here to rescue you, Jay—to look after your well-being, assuming that's what you want. This is all in keeping with the terms of my agreement with you and Jerry Jeris. But you seem to have an entirely different idea of my role in all of this that's erroneous. Speaking of roles, it's unclear to me exactly what *your* role is. Could you clear that up?"

"Shut your trap and get the hell in there!" Plankton snarled, moving away from the doorway to the back room, and waggling his large firearm at me.

"I guess we're going in there," I told Thad, and he followed me past Plankton, who kept the gun raised and his finger poised on the trigger.

The only illumination in the room was from the doorway we walked through. I could see that the windows had been covered with cardboard on which slogans had been spray-painted. One was *FFF Lives!* and another was *Queer Revenge!* It was a movie-of-the-week idea of gay protest, but someone must have thought it could be taken seriously by somebody.

The smell of nail polish was strong in the room, and it was apparent that here was the room where Leo Moyle had suffered his captivity. But as my eyes became accustomed to the gloom, who, I wondered, were the two figures bound and gagged on the couch in the darkest corner of the room? I was about to guess out loud when Thad beat me to it.

"Are you Miss Annette?" Thad said to the female, a bosomy, large-haired blond woman whose dark eyes were huge with fright. The other figure was that of a slender man in jeans and a white T-shirt, with thinning hair and black circles around his eyes, which also showed fear. Many tattoos adorned the man's arms, but I was unable to make out what they represented.

The scared woman was not able to answer Thad's question regarding her identity owing to the duct tape pasted across her lower face, and her eyes darted from the J-Bird to Thad to me and back to Plankton and his revolver.

"I'm starting to get the drift of what happened here," I said. "You're not actually party to a gigantic scam, Jay—unless you're a better actor than anybody I know is likely to give you credit for." Plankton's eyes narrowed as he tried to sort through that.

"Instead," I said, "it looks like your kidnapping was not a stunt that you knew anything about. You really were dragged out here against your will from New York and held here by these people and at least two others who aren't here right now. You managed to get loose from your bonds during the night, overpower these two, tie them up, and take possession of the revolver they had held on you and earlier on Leo Moyle.

"You were waiting for the other two members of the gang to return, at which point you would either notify the police, or—once you determined who was behind the operation, the FFF or someone else entirely—you would torment your tormentors for a time before deciding on their ultimate disposition. Am I right?"

"You're digging your own grave, Strachey," Plankton said. "But keep going."

"The part you're getting wrong, however, is this, Jay. Because you were blindfolded, you never saw your captors. When Thad and I walked through the front door just now instead of crashing through it, you assumed that we were the other two kidnap-gang members and that we had been part of an elaborate hoax from the beginning. Well, I'm here to tell you, Jay, that there has been a wicked hoax, yes. But Thad and I were never part of it. We're only here to expose the monstrous hoax and rescue you."

Plankton was shaking his head with a look of disgust. "What a pathetic wuss you are, Strachey. Christ, you don't even have the courage of your convictions." He indicated the graffiti on the cardboard window coverings, as if *Queer Revenge* figured importantly in my moral underpinnings. In fact, it ranked far down on my life's wish list, maybe number seven or eight.

I said, "Jay, you've been understandably unhinged by what you've been through. But before you miscalculate badly and randomly redistribute many of the human organs present in the room—and I *do* understand your impulse to do so—I want to point out a provable fact that is sure to come as an eye-opener to you."

Miss Annette's eyes got even bigger. She knew what was coming.

"Do you know, Jay, who this woman is?"

"Hell, she's some damn, man-hating, ball-breaking lipstick lesbian! Who gives a wet fart who she is?"

"No, you're wrong. Do you know where you are?"

"Shit, no. Where am I, anyway?"

"You're in Oyster Bay, Long Island, in an apartment over Annette Koontz's nail parlor. Miss Annette here is Steve Glodt's girlfriend. Why don't you remove the tape from across what I'm sure is her pretty mouth and ask her who organized and funded the kidnapping operation?"

Plankton stood there and said nothing for a long tense moment. You could see what was left of his operational mental machinery spinning fast. Finally, he said, "Say that again, Strachey?"

"Ask Miss Annette who had what to gain by making you and Leo even madder and meaner than you already are.

Ask her who is in negotiations with GSN for a radio-TV simulcast deal, only GSN wants more 'edge' on the show, more white male anger."

Plankton stood for a moment longer staring at me hard. Then he slowly turned his gaze toward Miss Annette. Her eyes stayed on the automatic, which turned toward her also.

"Is there any truth to that?" Plankton asked her, looking a little dazed now.

She nodded vigorously and said something that sounded like "Eee! Eee!" but was probably meant to be "Steve! Steve!"

Plankton stood for a moment longer. Then he sighed, lowered his gun, and said to Thad and me, "Come here. I want you to look at something."

He found a wall switch, and an overhead light went on. Still holding the automatic, Plankton rolled up his right sleeve. Freshly tattooed on his upper arm was a big heart, and inside it were the words J-Bird Loves Al Gore.

Thad said, "That looks bad, J-Bird. But it could have been worse."

"It was," Plankton said. Then he dropped his trousers, tugged at his boxer shorts, turned and bent over. Tattooed on his ample left buttock were the words "And J-Bird Loves"—and on his right buttock—"George W. Bush Even More."

Plankton yanked his pants up, the gun still in his right hand, and buckled his belt, the gun barrel wobbling dangerously.

"Glodt probably thought you'd think it was funny," I said.

"I don't."

"Apparently not."

Plankton pointed the gun again. "Come on. We're all going for a ride. The three of us, I mean."

"Why don't you let the police handle this, Jay? They're nearby. I can call them."

"Don't bother. I'll deal with Steve."

"We don't have a car," Thad said. "Somebody dropped us off."

Plankton looked at the tattooed man, who I assumed was Damien of Damien's Den of In-Ink-Kwity. "You got a car outside, you fucking pervert?"

The man nodded and thrust his right hip at us. "Get his keys," Plankton said.

I groped inside the man's pocket and came up with a set of keys.

"Which car is it?" I said. "The Rabbit?" He shook his head. "The Pontiac?" An eager assent—he wanted us out of there.

"Should I shoot these two before we go?" Plankton said, pointing his automatic, and this led to an outbreak of violent twisting and flopping on the couch. Plankton did not shoot, however. He just snorted and said, "Let's go see Steve. Steve wanted to deal with GSN, but first he's going to have to deal with me. Bring that box along," Plankton said, indicating an aluminum case the size of an airline carry-on bag that lay atop a nearby table. Then, wielding his gun again, Plankton motioned toward the door to the corridor. Thad and I did what the J-Bird seemed to want us to do, which was to lead the way out of Annette Koontz's apartment.

CHAPTER 24

I drove the old red Trans Am, Thad sat beside me in the passenger seat, and Plankton navigated from the backseat. He held the gun between and just behind our heads.

Thad said, "Do you know how to handle one of those shooters, J-Bird?"

"I do. You pull back on the trigger and the thing goes *blam, blam!*"

"Yep, I've heard that's how it works."

We wended our way out of the Oyster Bay commercial district and into a more residential area along Long Island Sound. Plankton was uncertain about where Steve Glodt's house was located. He had been there just once, he said, and he knew it was on something called Center Island, and you had to cross a small bridge to get there. We were unable to ask directions from anyone, what with the J-Bird constantly waving a gun around, so we took several wrong turns and had to backtrack to what Plankton believed was a correct route.

The roads were slick from the drizzle and patchy fog and I drove with the Pontiac's headlights on. Traffic was building up now, with drivers heading out to church or to pick up bagels and the Sunday papers. Leaving Oyster Bay, we passed a donut shop with a line of cars stretching around the building to the drive-up window.

Thad said, "J-Bird, couldn't you go for some donut holes? You must be famished."

"That can wait," was all Plankton said, and soon there were no more donut stores to tempt any of us.

I had my cellphone on my belt and said at one point, "Mind if I make a call, Jay? There are people who are going to wonder what's become of Thad and me."

"Let them wonder."

Minutes later we found Center Island. There was indeed a narrow bridge leading onto what even from the entrance to the enclave looked like a place where the shah of Iran might have kept a twenty-room hideaway and a helipad. The roofs of Georgian and Italianate palaces were visible through the trees in the distance.

A small guard outpost was at the end of the bridge we passed over, but there was no barrier, just a sign that said Turn Around Here.

"It's just local cops," Plankton said, lowering his gun for the moment. "Keep going. Don't even look at the cop house."

"So Center Island is not a gated community?" Thad said.

"These people don't need gates," Plankton said. "They're protected by the very fact of their money."

"It's not working in your case, J-Bird."

"No, it isn't."

We wound along a tree-lined road, where driveways,

some with wrought-iron gates, led off toward mansions whose rear terraces must have had glorious views of the water. I wondered if Annette Koontz had ever been out this way for a breezy afternoon sail followed by cocktails, but I supposed not.

I was hoping that Annette and Damien the tattooist had managed to free themselves and had gotten on the horn fast to warn Glodt what he might be in for. Not that I knew what Plankton had in mind or exactly what he was capable of, beyond the fetid gas-baggery so beloved by his radio fans. I did know that he had become enraged by what I had told him about Steve Glodt, and that he was carrying an automatic weapon I was afraid might be loaded.

"Slow down," Plankton said. "I think it's over there."

"That driveway?"

"Yeah, go left, in there."

It was probably the ugliest house on the island, a grotesque, recently built McMansion done in a hodgepodge of styles exemplifying the culture of waste, and no doubt on the site of some turn-of-the-century graceful marvel that hadn't been grandiose enough for Glodt. I almost wanted to ask Plankton for the gun so I could go in and shoot the media tycoon myself.

I parked at the top of the driveway in front of the three-car garage next to a forest-green Beemer convertible whose top was up against the drizzle.

"That's Steve's car," Plankton said. "The rabid weasel is in there."

I said, "Jay, we can't really be sure . . ."

"Get out," he said, pointing the gun, and Thad and I exited the Trans Am at the same time Plankton did.

"We'll go in through the garage," Plankton said, indicating a single closed door to the right of the three garage doors, which were shut tight, too.

"Go ahead," Plankton said, but when Thad tried to turn the doorknob, it wouldn't budge.

"It's locked," Thad said.

"Then I'll shoot it the fuck open."

"You don't have to," Thad said, getting out Dave Welch's Swiss Army knife.

"What's that?"

"I can probably do this lock with a corkscrew. But it might be alarmed. I'll bet every door and window on this island is alarmed."

"That doesn't matter. Go ahead. Open it."

Thad fooled around for half a minute, and then the door swung inward. I though I heard the beep-beep-beep of an alarm go off deep inside the hideous house.

"Go on in," Plankton said, and we entered the darkened garage, Thad, then me, then the J-Bird.

Plankton located a light switch to his right, flicked it on, and said, "Well, would you look at that fucker! That's the van they threw me into outside my apartment yesterday!"

The bay we were standing in was empty, as was the one on the far side of the garage. But in the middle bay, six feet away, was a light blue Dodge Ram.

A door leading into the house was suddenly flung open violently.

"Shit, it's him!" yelled a large young man in jeans and a tank top. He was followed by an even bigger, more muscular bruiser in an Oyster Bay Fitness Center T-shirt. As they lunged at the J-Bird, he fired a burst from his automatic, hitting one of the goons in the leg and then the other. They fell writhing and screaming onto the concrete floor.

I said, "Jay, unless you want to conduct your radio show from a cell at Attica from now on, we really need to call the police."

"Shut up." He motioned toward the door to the house. I went in, then Thad, and we found ourselves in a pantry anteroom off what looked like a large kitchen just ahead of us.

A lithe little man in designer jeans, a white silk shirt, and sockless loafers appeared in the kitchen door, and when he saw Thad and me and Plankton just behind us, the man went white and turned to run.

Blam! Blam! Blam! went the J-Bird's automatic. He had fired into the ceiling this time, but he yelled out, "Steve, you barf bag of blue puke! Get back here, or I'll blast your prostate right through your shriveled liver and out the other side!"

Though anatomically unlikely, this threat stopped Glodt in his tracks, and he turned back toward us, his hands jabbing at the air above him. "Jay, don't shoot me! Jay, really, it was all in your own best interests. It was all for your career, Jay. For the show. Let's talk. Let me explain. Now you've fucked it up, of course, to a certain extent. But let's salvage what we can. Come on in, let me fix some Bloody Marys . . ."

Blam! Blam! The gun went off again, this time blasting a gaping hole in a cupboard door. In addition to the cordite, the smells I could make out were vacuum-packed Alaskan smoked salmon and dill sauce.

"Pick up that phone!" Plankton ordered Glodt.

His arms still in the air, Glodt pointed daintily with one finger at a wall phone and said, "That phone? Who do you want me to call, Jay?"

"Call the Center Island cops and tell them not to respond to the alarm. They're probably on their way out here now, so apologize, give them the code, and tell them how embarrassed you are that your Salvadoran maid's stupid six-year-old brat set off the alarm."

"Can I remember all that? You've got me so fucking nervous."

"Do it! Now!"

Glodt did as he was instructed, while Plankton held the big gun three feet from Glodt's face.

When Glodt hung up the phone and reached for the sky again, Plankton said, "Who else is in the house? Is your wife here?"

"No, nobody's here, Jay, so let's talk. Sheila's in the city and it's the maid's day off. Jay, what'd you do to Ken and Wally? Do they need medical attention? I can understand why you're pissed, but . . . well, hey, that's the point! Get it? You're pissed, and you're gonna stay pissed, I'm sure, and . . ."

"Get inside!" Plankton barked, waving the gun again. "Go on!"

Glodt edged his way into the kitchen, and we followed. The rear of the large room had a wide window, and misty Long Island Sound spread away grayly in the distance.

"Is Annette okay?" Glodt said. "You didn't shoot Annette, did you, Jay? Please tell me you didn't whack Annette."

Plankton did not answer Glodt's question. Instead, he said to Thad, "Go out to the car and get the case. Come right back in, 'cause if you don't I'm gonna blow Strachey's nuts off. And check on those two bozos on the garage floor. See if I need to come back out there and plug 'em in the gut."

Thad shot me a quick glance, then went out. Plankton peered around the kitchen, a culinary Taj Mahal of polished granite and gleaming brass with a sink-and-counter island in the center. "We'll set up over there," the J-Bird said, indicating a marble-top aluminum-frame breakfast table with four aluminum chairs next to the big window. "Sit down," Plankton told Glodt, who promptly complied.

Thad was back within seconds with the aluminum case we had carried out of Annette Koontz's apartment. Thad said, "The two men you shot in the leg, J-Bird, are alive, but they need an ambulance, in my opinion. One's semiconscious and they're both bleeding."

"If they need to go to the hospital, they can walk," Plankton said. "Tell me, Steve, are those two on the garage floor a couple of the goons who snatched me from in front of my apartment yesterday?"

Screwing up his face, Glodt affected a look of concerned contrition. "They didn't hurt you, did they, Jay? They're just a couple of zit-heads who work for a guy in Garden City I borrowed money from one time when I had a personal-debt type of situation, and I was well aware when I took these dorks on that it would not have been to your advantage or mine if you had been injured in any way. I made myself one thousand percent clear on that particular score. I just want to be sure you understand that. Anyway, it was just like if those FFF assholes had been the ones who did it. Except *those* cocksuckers might really have roughed you up, and *we* were nice to you, and in fact we were actually going to let you go this afternoon.

"Jesus, if you'd just been a little more patient, Jay, you'd have been back in Babette's pussy by tonight, and the whole deal would have paid off big time for me and you and Leo and Jerry and all of us. Except, no, you had to go all macho on me and grab Annette's gun I gave her to protect her against the beaners moving into Oyster Bay, and then you come charging over here like some Jersey wise guy, kapowee, kapowee, kapowee. But it's not too late, you know, Jay? Knowing what you know, perhaps it would be appropriate, like, if you got a bigger slice of the GSN deal. Would that smooth things over between us? I'll bet my left devil dog it'd go a long way toward making things right, am I right?"

Plankton stood staring at Glodt, his red eyes full of fury. Somewhere along the way he had lost his shades, and his wrecked mug was not a pretty sight without them.

"Explain this to me, Steve," Plankton said, ignoring Glodt's entreaties. "On WINS they were saying my tongue was ripped out and sent to the *Post*. Fortunately, that was a fat, stupid lie. Whose tongue was it you sent over there, anyway?"

Glodt tried to chuckle, but the sound he made contained more desperation than amusement. He said, "It was a sheep's tongue. Ken found it in a Middle Eastern butcher shop in Jersey City. The cops would have figured it out, but by then you'd've been freed and back on the air, anyway. Your loyal fan base would've known you still had a tongue to flap—and of course Babette would have known it, too, heh heh heh."

Plankton was pondering something. "Jerry wasn't in on this, was he?"

"What do you think?"

"Just answer my question before I shoot your black heart across your backyard and across the sound to Norwalk!"

"No, no, Jerry didn't know! He was sick about the whole thing. He even got me to raise the reward money to six-five. I just used Jerry, picking up information on the police investigation, and on some PI from Albany that was involved, and some Amish queen from the FFF that we tried to make it look like he was involved in the snatch. I'm sure Jerry would've gone along with it if he knew, but the way I did it was even better. Don't you get it, J-Bird? It would only really work perfectly if you all were sincerely distraught and ripshit."

Plankton considered carefully what he had heard. Then he said to Thad and me, "Tie him down. I want him stretched over the table, butt end up, and tied tight. Find some rope, or some neckties in his bedroom."

"Hey, wait a minute . . . !"

Blam! Blam! Blam! The gun went off again, smashing a shelf full of what looked like Venetian fruit bowls. The far side of the kitchen was a rainbow of flying Murano.

I said, "I'll go look in the garage for something to tie him up with."

"No, you won't," Plankton said. "I don't trust you for shit, Strachey. I didn't trust you from the second I laid eyes on you, you being some limp-wristed Albany fairy. Use those electrical cords," Plankton said, waving his gun at some extension cords, one leading to a lamp on a phone table, another to a television set mounted on a metal wall shelf. "Those'll work. Tie him down with those cords."

Glodt, on whom the automatic was trained, looked frantic. "Jay, what are you going to do?"

"You'll see."

"You're not going to rape me, are you, Jay?"

"Not exactly."

"Jay, I think you're losing it. You're not the J-Bird I thought I knew."

"Do it!" Plankton snapped at Thad and me.

It took four extension cords, including two Thad retrieved from the pantry, for us to tightly secure Glodt's feet to the legs of one side of the table and his wrists to the other. Glodt had begun to whimper. He had no idea what he was in for, though by now I was beginning to think I did.

"Get the case," Plankton said calmly.

I picked up the aluminum case Thad had brought in from the car and placed it on a nearby chair.

"Open it," Plankton said.

I unsnapped the latches and lifted the lid.

"Pull his pants down," Plankton said, and Glodt let out a scream.

Thad said, "What is that thing, an electric nose-hair trimmer, or what? Are you going to shave his butt-hole or something, J-Bird? Look, I have to tell you, this is getting to be a bit more than I can stomach. Honestly."

"What you're looking at," Plankton said, motioning toward the contents of the case, "is a tattoo gun along with its inks and accessories. I was blindfolded at the time, so I can't say for sure. But my guess is, this is the tattoo gun that that fruitcake in Oyster Bay used to desecrate the holy temple of my crumbling, pathetic, middle-aged body. And now, Steve, your holy temple is about to be desecrated, too."

Glodt screamed again and began to struggle violently. Plankton stepped closer to Glodt and shoved the barrel of the automatic against Glodt's right temple. Glodt froze in place but almost immediately began to shake all over.

"Strachey, you can do the honors. If you refuse, I'll blow Steve's brains out. If you think I'm bluffing, go ahead and test me."

"I've never used one of these things," I said.

"You can experiment. On Steve."

"I took your basic Introduction to Art History in college, but I have no artistic talent myself."

"You won't need any. This doesn't have to be perfect. Anyway, it's pretty much all text."

"I thought it might be."

"Plug it in."

"I might need another extension cord."

"Thad, find another cord." Thad glanced at me again, and I nodded. I was beginning to understand that everyone in the room would almost certainly survive the day uninjured and largely intact.

Plankton confirmed this by saying, "Tattoo what I tell you to write on Steve's butt. Then I'll put the gun down and you can call the cops. But if you don't do it, I'll kill Steve. Deal?"

"Deal," I said.

Glodt mewed softly as I loosened his belt and tugged his jeans and undershorts down in the back.

Thad returned with another extension cord and plugged one end into a wall socket near the coffeemaker. The other end I attached to the tattoo gun. The device resembled a large hypodermic syringe with a needle in the end. When I flicked a switch, the needle vibrated.

I said, "These little jars appear to contain ink. What color would you like, J-Bird? Or should I ask Steve?"

"Blue would be good," Plankton said. "It was good enough for me, and it will be good enough for Steve."

I removed the lid from a jar of dark blue ink. With the tattoo gun poised above Glodt's buttocks—which were remarkably firm and well-preserved for a man who was probably in his early fifties—I said to Plankton, "What is it, J-Bird, that you would like me to write?"

He told me, and Glodt began to sob.

Thad said, "That's cruel, J-Bird. That's sick."

"Do it, or I'll kill him. It's not as cruel and sick as murder."

I thought he was probably bluffing, but he spoke with such cold rage that I wasn't sure. In any case, I figured Glodt could have the tattoos removed—slowly, painfully— before they could bring him any greater harm.

"I should sketch this out first," I said, "so that I do the job as neatly as possible. Is there a marker or something?"

Thad brought a felt-tipped pen from the telephone table. He wasn't trembling, nor did he have goose bumps. But his face was taut and pale, and I could see in his eyes that he was suffering. Thad's early days as a daring FFF rescuer must have seemed so innocent and larky next to this, and I didn't doubt that he would soon head back to his eggplants and moody lover and orderly extended gay-and-lesbian family and never again head off on some midlife adventure that the likes of people like me had lured him into.

I took the pen and carefully wrote on Glodt's perspiring left buttock: "Queen of the New York State Correctional System." Then on his left cheek I drew an arrow pointing to Glodt's anus, and the words "Enter Here."

It took me a few minutes to develop a feel for using the gun and when and how to dip the needle in the ink jars. So I made a few blotchy mistakes. But when I finished the job an hour or so later, it wasn't bad overall, and the J-Bird complimented me on my work.

Then I made some phone calls, and soon after that two ambulances arrived, along with a Center Island police cruiser. At almost the same moment, Lyle Barner and Dave Welch glided up the Glodt driveway.

Glodt was still draped over the kitchen table when Lyle

and Welch came in, Lyle's police special drawn. The J-Bird had laid down his automatic by then, and Lyle soon lowered his.

Welch said, "Hey, nice butt."

Taking note of the J-Bird, Lyle said to Welch, "What are you, queer or something? Now, what the hell is going on here, Strachey? It looks to me as if you have a lot of explaining to do."

Welch shook his head, Thad raised an eyebrow, the J-Bird snorted, and Steve Glodt said, "Are you police officers? Thank God you're here! I've been attacked and held prisoner by these radical homosexual activists! Apparently they are the same deranged perverts who kidnapped my friend and full business partner, Jay Plankton here, who luckily was able to escape from his sadistic captors!"

There was a pause while we all looked over at the J-Bird, who suddenly let loose with a ferocious cackle.

CHAPTER 25

Midnight Sunday in Albany. The rain had moved out but not the heat and humidity, and when I stepped off the train I felt as though I was breathing peanut butter. I had picked up the *Times* at Penn Station and thought the Sunday crossword puzzle would represent a wholesome change of mental pace. But I dozed off before the train had cleared the tunnel heading north from midtown, and if the conductor hadn't wakened me—"Hey, young fella, Albany's your stop, isn't it?"—I might have remained unconscious right through to Cleveland.

Timothy Callahan was there at the Rensselaer Amtrak station to bring me home, and a happy sight was Timmy.

"Donald, you're not looking your freshest."

"No, but you are, by and large. Lucky me."

"You did a fine job, and all your exertions paid off nicely. And even though Lyle Barner was involved, you didn't get your ear chewed off this time, or apparently anything else, either."

"Nope, I'm in one piece."

"And with the vast wealth of these media heavies at your disposal, I take it you've been—or soon will be—amply rewarded."

We found Timmy's car in the Amtrak lot and climbed into it. I rolled the window down and said, "Yeah, I'll get paid. I think."

"There's doubt? Donald, not again."

"Oh, I'll squeeze it out of them. I know too much."

"Too much of what? I saw on CNN that Jay Plankton was rescued, and this Glodt guy who owns the radio network was behind it all, and that you were involved in finding Plankton, and Glodt is in custody. There's more?"

We pulled out onto the street leading to the bridge across the Hudson. I said, "Glodt briefly talked Plankton into saying the whole thing was a gag, and that I was in on it from the beginning, and if I said otherwise publicly, they would label me some humorless PC asshole and sue me for defamation of character."

"What rot. And spectacularly unbelievable."

"It was. Plankton loved the sound of it, and there were ratings and big bucks in it for him and Steve Glodt, but Plankton soon saw that it could never work. Lyle and this other New York cop had seen and heard way too much, and anyway there were too many people involved in the conspiracy—two of them shot in the leg by Plankton—and these people were sure to turn against the masterminds of the plot in return for a better deal from the prosecutors. Glodt was going down, and the J-Bird soon saw that. He had no interest in going down, too."

"What a scuzzy bunch of people."

"They're bad, all right."

"Well, now you've paid off your debt to Lyle, Don. If he ever asks you again to get mixed up with reprobates like the J-Bird, you can say, 'Sorry, old pal,' with a clear conscience."

"That's my plan. Though I'm not sure Lyle will be calling on me again. I'm still an embarrassment to him. After all these years."

"What, your being out?"

"It has to be hard for gay cops."

"It is. Whether they're in or out, it's no picnic. The out cops get beat up on, and the nonout cops beat up on themselves. I admire all of them, but I don't envy them. Not one bit."

As we cruised across the Dunn Bridge, the Albany skyline spread out against the murk ahead of us, Timmy said, "They said on the news that Glodt had asked for both a lawyer and a dermatologist. What was that about?"

"Oh my. Was he allowed access to a dermatologist?"

"A judge was considering the request, CNN said. What's the problem? Did Glodt have some kind of violent skin reaction to his arrest? Hysterical acne or something?"

I thought, should I tell him? Timmy wasn't going to appreciate my role in this. But this was important—or would have been considered important, I knew, by the everlasting Jesuit Callahan. He would need to parse the moral complexities before eliciting statements from me into which he could read a degree of contrition, prior to conferring conditional absolution on me in the recesses of his mind.

Anyway, as I described it all to Timmy, I made it plain that I had no choice in the matter. It was either carry out the tattoo job or Plankton just might blow Glodt's head apart.

Timmy accepted my explanation with unexpected equanimity. He just said, "Wow. You spent an hour writing on this guy's naked butt."

"I did. I fantasized about you, of course."

"Did he have a nice one?"

"It wasn't bad at all."

"What did Thad Diefendorfer make of all this?"

"He was revolted."

"What a sweet guy he is. I hope we see him again."

"We will. He and his partner and their lesbian house-mates are coming for a visit with their little kid in August. Thad thinks they'd all like to visit the Berkshire llamas, if not suck the cheese."

As we turned onto Crow Street, Timmy said, "If you wanted to, you could pay your respects to Jay Plankton again, too. On CNN about an hour ago the J-Bird said he planned on setting up a camp, probably in the Berkshires, where the victims of kidnappings could go for counseling and rest and rehabilitation. On his radio show tomorrow he's going to ask listeners for contributions to establish the camp. And he's arranging to have at least twelve of the Iran U.S. Embassy hostages on the show this month. And then he's going to broadcast future shows from Colombia and the Philippines, where there are lots of what he called 'cruel and tragic kidnappings similar to my own and Leo Moyle's.' Americans will be able to see all this on television too, the J-Bird said, when simulcasting begins in the fall on the Gonzo Sports Network."

But of course. "I'll say this much for Plankton," I told Timmy. "He's a vile sham, but he's nimble."

"The kidnap victims' rehab camp," Timmy added, "is going to be called Camp Babette, after Plankton's fiancée. Oh, and the Bush campaign is going to make a cash contri-bution to the camp, and if Bush is elected, they said he'll be there for the grand opening."

"At least we don't have to sweat that," I said. "Gore's got it nailed."

Timmy parked the car and said, "Come on in the house, and maybe if I work at it I can talk you into writing mes-sages on me for a change."

I said it wouldn't take much.

only lib owning this!

ˣ8

9/03

BAKER & TAYLOR